Words of praise for Toni Sorenson Brown and the Shirley You Can Do It! Books

"The SHIRLEY YOU CAN DO IT! books offer a realistic, warm-hearted approach to everyday living, with a twist of humor that is uniquely Toni Brown. I love a book that has me laughing and crying . . . all on the same page. Toni's books will move you to that, page after page." —Marie Osmond

"It is a small treasure with a large impact. It can be read in one evening and savored for many nights to come . . . VALIDATE ME QUICK is like finding a new friend that understands how the daily frustrations of life can sometimes become overwhelming." —*Davis County Clipper* (Utah)

"Witty and captivating . . . Recommended to all those weary moms and wives who feel they are lacking appreciation."
—*Horizon News* (Salt Lake City, Utah)

"Until now, there has never been a series of books written especially for women by a woman. The idea is a singular one in a saturated market . . . As the readers get to know Shirley, they will discover that they know a little bit more about themselves. Her powerful, humorous messages have a universal appeal to all women." —*Park City's E.A.R.* (Utah)

"The well-placed humor and reaffirming quality of the work make it appealing . . . an entertaining book about self-discovery and the female experience . . . the perfect gift for any woman."
—*Salt Lake Observer*

The Shirley You Can Do It! Books from Toni Sorenson Brown and St. Martin's Paperbacks

Validate Me Quick; I'm Double-Parked!

In My Quest for Personal Growth, the Rest of Me Grew, Too!

Check the Lost and Found, My Mind is Missing!

Check the Lost And Found My Mind is Missing!

(Previously published as *'Tis the Season . . . To Go Crazy!*)

Toni Sorenson Brown

St. Martin's Paperbacks

Check the Lost and Found, My Mind Is Missing! was previously published under the title *'Tis the Season . . . to Go Crazy!*

CHECK THE LOST AND FOUND, MY MIND IS MISSING!

Library of Congress Catalog Card Number: 96-71674

ISBN: 0-312-97090-0

Printed in the United States of America

Token Ink edition / November 1996
St. Martin's Paperbacks edition / October 2000

10 9 8 7 6 5 4 3 2 1

For

Jennifer Enderlin and Jan Miller,
women of faith, courage and vision.
I will forever be in your debt.

Out of the strain of Doing, into the peace of the Done.

—Julia Louise Woodruff

Check the Lost
And Found
My Mind is
Missing!

One

The remains of the day.

Yuck.

Just hours before, this mangled mess had resembled dinner. Edible. Delectable. A real Thanksgiving feast. Now Shirley slumped across the table from a mountain of dried out cranberry sauce and congealed gravy. Plates stuck together between layers of mashed sweet potatoes and mutilated black olives. The olives had served earlier as finger puppets for the children, including her *biggest* child—her husband, Stan. Stan was the one who had first taught her how ten medium-sized pitted black olives could come to life, five as pilgrims, the other five as Indians. How many years had Shirley watched her beloved spouse puppeteer the story of Thanksgiving, only to devour the entire cast as soon as the play was concluded?

The Thanksgiving bird of honor now loomed across Shirley's only silver serving platter, like an abandoned carcass on the African plain. A skeletal heap, picked over by the scavengers. Bon appétit, Butterball.

The mess was enough to depress anybody. Shirley propped her elbows on the table and silently cursed herself for being the one who always insisted on this annual ritual. Every year since she and Stan had been married, well over a decade now, Shirley had bid a Thanksgiving welcome to *all*. Her family. His family. The lonely people from their church. One year Stan had even brought a homeless family in to dine with them. At least that year she knew what to do with the leftovers.

Thanksgiving was never dull, that was for sure. She recalled the year that Stan's grandfather and Shirley's great-aunt had recognized each other from a long-ago romance—that chance encounter had really set the excitement precedent. Shirley couldn't remember for certain—was it her great-uncle who had thrown the first punch? After that fiasco, this year would surely go down in the family folklore books as a dud.

Now that everyone had gone home, and Stan and the kids were slouched in front of the TV watching a video, a peaceful contentment slowly filled Shirley's heart. She stuck her finger into a leftover pie, then licked whipped cream and spiced pumpkin.

"This is my idea of heaven." She sighed aloud. "The rumors are true—I *am* nuts."

"What are you saying?" Stan shouted from the adjacent family room.

"I was just talking to the turkey," she replied.

"I thought you might be complaining about nobody helping you clean up the mess."

"What if I was?"

Stan took his time in responding. "I would be right by your side. I just don't understand why you never let our mothers help you clean up. You always resolve to do it solo."

"I realize you don't understand, Stanley. Did you know that in some families the women prepare the Thanksgiving meal, then the men do all of the cleanup, while the women watch football?"

Stan suddenly appeared behind her, massaging her shoulders. "*What* families?"

"I heard about them on a talk show," she confessed.

"Figures. That's where you get most of your facts. How would you feel if next year Sean and Stephen and I were in charge of cooking Thanksgiving dinner?"

Shirley reached up and took his hand. "Stephen is a baby. Sean can't pour milk into a glass without spilling it. As you for," she said, elbowing him in the ribs, "you grill a mean hot dog, but I don't think hot dogs would please your mother's Thanksgiving pallet."

He shrugged. "How about TV dinners?"

Shirley shook her head. "No, even Swanson can't cook to please your mother."

"What could my mom possibly have to complain about"—he smiled—"that the meat was dry, the potatoes needed more salt, and the rolls were too heavy?"

Shirley had to return his smile. "That's exactly what she said about today's meal. I didn't realize you were paying attention to the annual critique."

"I hope you know my mother means well. She would never hurt your feelings on purpose."

Shirley felt the muscles in her shoulders tighten. She pulled back from Stan's touch. Shirley loved her mother-in-law, but the woman was not a subject she and Stan could ever talk about without Shirley feeling stressed and beaten.

"Do you want me to help you with the dishes?" Stan whispered.

"Sure," she replied, knowing very well that he was expecting her to pass on his offer. She stood, handing Stan a stack of dirty dishes that he obediently carried to the kitchen sink.

"Anything else?"

"You can carve the rest of the turkey and take care of the carcass. You can put the remainder of the food in Tupperware containers and organize them in the refrigerator. You can scrape the plates and load the dishwasher. You can scrub the pots and pans and mop the floor. You can—"

"Okay, okay." Stan grabbed another load of plates and deposited them on the counter. Then he looked into the family room and announced, "I think little Stephen is waking up. I'd better go check on him."

Shirley nodded. She knew her husband. Stan was never going to be Mister Mom. She attributed it to his upbringing, and excused him, because he once confessed that he was terrified of being the "yes-man" he considered his father to be.

Shirley thought of herself as an extremely lenient wife, supportive to a fault. She enjoyed watching Stan play out the part he described as "an independent *manly* man." He could act just about any way he wanted, pursue any dream, just as long as he never confused her role. She was his wife—*not* his mother. Every once in a while he seemed to forget that, and crossed into some dangerous and confused territory.

Whenever the comparison between Shirley and her mother-in-law reared its ugly head, Shirley found a way to redefine her role. She bunched up the tablecloth, along with all the bits of spilled food, and thought to herself: *Stan—Tarzan. Shirley—Jane. Mother-in-law—Cheetah.* No, no. Just kidding. Her feelings were embedded deeper than she thought. Maybe after the holidays she would make an appointment with a shrink. There were issues to be addressed. Lots and lots of issues. While her mother-in-law was involved in a few of them, Stan in many, her own mother was Mother-of-All-Issues.

This particular evening, Shirley decided to set issues aside, and simply allowed herself to be thankful for all that she had. Stan was a good man, that was something Shirley found too easy to forget, but times like this, when he ran from the kitchen like a terrified little boy, and headed for the couch where he cuddled his infant son, Stan and his vulnerability topped her list of "Reasons to Give Thanks."

As soon as the dishwasher was loaded, the food in the fridge and the floor swept, Shirley joined her family in front of the television. She collapsed on the sofa next to Stan and the baby. The rest of the kids were sprawled around the room. They were halfway through watching Jimmy Stewart discover what Shirley had felt all day.

She snuggled closer to Stan.

"You're in a good mood," he said with a twinge of surprise.

"I'm feeling nostalgic," she admitted. "There's something about Thanksgiving night that makes me feel a little sentimental."

"There's something about Thanksgiving night that makes me feel a little hungry," he responded.

Shirley pulled away and sat upright. She looked at him. "You're joking, right?"

"No. A turkey sandwich with all the fixings sounds pretty good to me."

"Me, too!" Seven-year-old Sean suddenly emerged from the rug in front of the TV. "I want a turkey sandwich, with no cranberries."

"Is there any more fruit salad left?" asked Samantha, who was thirteen and had been excused from helping with the cleanup only because right after dinner she had claimed to have one of those mysterious teenage girl ailments—something about aching all over, feeling icky, and not wanting to *accidentally* sneeze on the food.

Shirley glanced across the room at her firstborn, who was in the middle of applying the umpteenth coat of magenta nail polish to her toenails. Samantha looked the picture of health to Shirley.

"I want some pumpkin pie with extra whipped cream," ordered Sara, pumping the rocking chair with her bare heels.

"Oh, you do, do you?" Shirley said. "For a four-year-old, you really know how to bark orders."

"And I want milk, too," Sara added unabashedly.

Shirley snorted. "Didn't you people just stuff yourselves with enough food to last a grizzly through hibernation? Now that I have it all cleaned up and put away, you're ready to start again?"

As if on cue, baby Stephen started to squirm. Stan handed him to Shirley. "I think he's hungry," Stan surmised, "and he could use a changing."

Shirley cleared her throat loudly, sounding more irritated than she actually felt. "Don't all of you jump up at once to help me. You might strain one of those muscles you've been relaxing."

Stan reached forward to retrieve Stephen. "I'm joking. Fix a baby bottle and I'll feed him. I'll even change him if you'll hand me a diaper and some wipes."

"You've got yourself a deal."

Stan pressed his lips to Stephen's tiny pudgy fist and waved it at Shirley, like a pleading puppet. "And a turkey sandwich?"

"*And* a turkey sandwich," Shirley relented. "Anybody care to help me?"

Her family instantly appeared very engrossed in the angel Clarence's plight. Would he get his wings or not?

Shirley grunted, went to the refrigerator, and muttered to the neatly packaged and stacked remnants of the day, "It's a wonderful life, all right."

Two

Shirley's spirits were not dampened for long. The next morning she was up before the rest of the family to greet one of her favorite days of the year—the beginning of the Christmas season. She refused to officially begin the season until the day *after* Thanksgiving. Despite the commercialism of the holidays, and the fact that the local malls had been decorated since *before* Halloween this year, Shirley had been brought up to believe there was something sacrilegious about tackling the observance too soon.

Every year she intended to shop the after-Christmas sales, in preparation for the following year, but she just never got around to it. By the time Christmas was over, she was too drained—emotionally and financially.

This year, she vowed, would be different. This year she would actually *enjoy* the holidays. This year she would get her shopping done early. She would stick to her budget. Out-of-town gifts would be mailed the first week in December. The annual family Christmas card photo still needed to be taken. *That,* she had put off on purpose, hoping that she could lose a few more pounds before the post office declared her time for mailing greetings expired. Oh well, she might just send out a snapshot of the children. Everyone had been asking for a photo of the new baby, but she couldn't think of a single person who had requested a current photo of *her* smiling mug.

The Christmas tree needed to be purchased and decorated right away. This year a living tree was her contribution to saving the environment. The lights had to be strung and the decorations put up. Maybe this year Stan would actually hang the outside lights they had bought the first year of their marriage.

Every year he vowed he would hang them, but never found the time. It was always too cold and the roof was always too high. There were a few years when Shirley had threatened to hire someone else to hang their outside lights, but Stan talked her out of it, saying, "I have a plan for those lights. I want to put them all around the dormers and really make a statement." In the meantime, Shirley wondered if she could even find them, should Stan suddenly have the urge to honor promises and ascend to the rooftop.

Shirley's mind was flooded with the anticipation and preparation of the holidays. There were parties, presents, and people that epitomized the season, and she was looking forward to all of them.

To get the holidays underway, Shirley put on Stan's battered audio tape of the Mormon Tabernacle Choir's holiday favorites. Then she poured some cinnamon oil into a saucepan and set it on the stove to simmer. Homemade potpourri.

The telephone rang. It was Stan's boss, Curtis. Not a good omen. He had to hold the line a good five minutes before Shirley was able to shake Stan from his vacation slumber.

"It's my day off," he moaned. "Tell Curtis that I'm sleeping."

"He knows you're sleeping; that's why he told me to wake you. Still, I almost didn't. You looked like you were in the middle of *some* dream!"

"I was dreaming I actually had a day off without that jerk calling to bug me." Stan rolled over and reached for the telephone on the nightstand next to the bed.

Shirley knew this scenario all too well. She knew that Stan was miserable working under his new boss; Curtis was a self-righteous cretin. But how was Stan supposed to walk away from a dozen years at the same company? Starting over in your twenties was exciting, but when you were nearly double that age and beginning anew, it was the most terrifying thought in the world. Shirley's heart went out to Stan. He was a good husband and provider, and she wanted to see him happy, but she didn't want to risk their family's security on a new job venture. Maybe she was the only one who was afraid of starting over. *No, not me,* she mused. *I never really got my career started in the first place.*

Shirley shook her head. Too many negative thoughts for a day like today. She would worry about job satisfaction and new horizons after the holidays. Today she simply wanted to enjoy the day. She was determined to launch the Christmas season with a bang. No negative thinking, she reprimanded herself, kissing Stan's cheek, whispering, "It's going to be okay. Whatever Curtis wants, just tell him no!"

Stan rolled his eyes and shot her a look of frustrated defeat.

A few minutes later when he came down the stairs, Shirley had the table set with red and green candles as Christmas centerpieces.

"They make the Cheerios look more festive," she joked, attempting to solicit a smile from her husband.

No such luck. The gloom on his face made it clear that his day off had ended before it had begun. "I've got to go into the office this morning. Seems Curtis wants some help to finish *his* proposal to that Japanese company."

For one brief moment Shirley was angry with Stan. This day was a *family* ritual! No work. Just play. How dare he defile this day-after-Thanksgiving tradition!

Shirley's anger dissipated as quickly as it arrived. She realized it was misdirected. She should be angry at Curtis, the parasitic boss from hell. Besides, Stan acted angry enough for both of them. Shirley looked into her husband's eyes, and knew that he felt just as disappointed, just as deflated as she did.

"I hope I can be home by noon," he said without much conviction.

"The stores stay open late tonight, so that might still work," she offered. "We can all go shopping when you get finished at work."

Stan sighed. "You might as well just go without me. I know how you don't like to shop, but today's the one day you wanna be there when the stores open for the big sales."

He was right, Shirley wasn't much of a shopper, but today was an exception. "Maybe I'll pack up all the kids and go to the mall this morning. I've been working on my shopping list, and this year, I've decided to get everything finished and out of the way so we can just relax and enjoy the season."

Stan put two pieces of bread into the toaster and waited until they had popped up and were lathered with grape jelly. "Have a bite," he offered Shirley.

"No, thanks," she declined.

"Bah, humbug to you, too," was his only reply.

Three

As soon as Stan left for his office, Shirley blew out the festive candles and dialed her friend Rita's telephone number. She had met Rita a few months back, just before Stephen was born. The two had become fast friends, giving credence to the adage that opposites attract. In Shirley's mind, Rita was everything Shirley was *not*.

Rita was rich. She was eloquent. She was traveled. She was impeccable in her appearance. Shirley once went shopping with her, and realized that Rita spent more on a single outfit than Shirley did on a month's worth of groceries. Granted, the ensemble included matching shoes and a purse, but still, the thought of spending so much on clothes made Shirley dizzy with guilt.

Rita was thin. Pencil-thin. Maybe that justified spending so much on her wardrobe. When you looked that good in a size five, why not?

Shirley was a little envious, although she would never admit it aloud. *What would it be like to swap lives with Rita just for a day?* Shirley often wondered. Ah, to be too skinny, too rich, too classy—what a fantasy! It ranked right up there with her vision of being a successful psychologist, rescuing people from their troubles with a single word of advice. Someday she would put her psychology degree to good use, but for now, she was mesmerized by Rita's grace and elegance as she lifted the lives of the downtrodden.

Rita was devoted to her career. She arranged financing for women's causes—everything from women's shelters to the rehabilitation program at the state correctional facility. Rita was obsessed with helping women in need. Her drive and endless motivation were still puzzling to Shirley. There was something behind Rita's obsession with helping women in need, but Shirley was still unraveling that mystery.

There were a lot of mysterious aspects about Rita that drove Shirley crazy. The woman was a closed book. Shirley was gradually beginning to read her, feeling more and more grateful for their friendship. Just being around Rita made Shirley want to do more with her own life. Someday, Shirley vowed, she would be more than an observer. But not now; now she was too busy merely coping with the mundane. Just the thought of all that she wanted to accomplish, compared to what she managed to accomplish, sent a shudder of guilt though her soul.

Rita was not driven by emotions like Shirley. Shirley ran on pure emotions—mainly guilt. Rita, on the other hand, let her head rule her life. She moved with purpose, direction. She managed to stay focused. She made a list of things to do and had each item checked off in red marker before retiring for the night. Rita called it "prioritizing."

At the moment, Shirley's priority was to get to the mall before all of the good stuff was ransacked.

When Rita didn't answer the telephone, Shirley figured she must be out saving the world. So Shirley went upstairs and woke her pubescent daughter, Samantha.

"Rise and shine. It's Christmas time!"

Samantha rolled over and burrowed her face in her pillow.

"Get up, sleepyhead. I need your help."

"Aw, Mom. I don't feel so great. I've got a stomachache."

"That's too bad, because I'm going to the mall this morning."

The pillow flew into the air, billowing the sheet atop Shirley's head. Samantha was out of bed in an instant, standing in front of the closet.

"What am I going to wear?"

"I don't know, but I know I'm not wearing *this*." Shirley laughed, untangling herself from the forsaken bedding. "I washed your new jeans, the shredded ones with the holes in the knees. They're in the laundry room."

"Cool. Have you seen my red sweater?"

"It's there, too."

"Thanks, Mom. Can I call my friend Heather to see if she wants to come with us?"

"If you think she's willing to help tend the kids while I do some Christmas shopping."

Samantha looked as though someone had just stolen her best

piece of Halloween candy. "*Tend*? You mean I have to baby-sit at the mall?"

Shirley nodded vigorously.

"But Sean is such a brat. Sara whines all the time, and what if Stephen needs to be changed? I'm not changing diapers at the mall."

"We can take both strollers and trade off. If the baby needs to be changed, I'll do it."

"What about Dad? Why can't he at least tend Sean?"

"Because your father had to go into work today."

"I thought he had the day off. This was supposed to be a *family* day."

"I know, I know. But Curtis called, and your father had to go help him with a project."

"That guy's a geek. Dad should just learn to say no."

"I think your Dad wishes he could."

"Why doesn't he?"

"Because Curtis is his boss. You don't tell your boss no."

"I would."

"I'm sure you would, my naive unemployed teenager. Now get dressed, and I'll go wake up Sean and Sara."

After a quick breakfast of Cheerios with green milk (Sean's food-color contribution to the festive color scheme), the family piled in the minivan and headed to the mall. They arrived a half an hour before the stores opened, but even then, parking places were about as scarce as a chocolate-sprinkled donut at a policeman's convention.

"This is ridiculous," Shirley complained, circling the parking lot for the third time. Finally, she decided to let the children out by the front door, determining she would have to park next to a snow bank at the far end of the parking lot, the only available space big enough to accommodate the van. "That way I won't have to drag the stroller and you kids across a half mile of filth and sludge," she explained to a whining Samantha. "Now wait right by the front door. Don't go anywhere else. I'll meet you there in five minutes."

When Shirley trudged across the parking lot, through the snow and crowds, she was horrified to find the children were not by the door. They were nowhere in sight. No sign of Samantha or the strollers. No Sean. No Sara. No Stephen. She looked around at the ocean of rippling people and wondered where to start searching. How could two strollers and four children disappear in a matter of minutes?

She peered around. Not one person even remotely resembled mall security, but everyone suddenly looked suspiciously like mass murderers.

Shirley couldn't help it. The kids were missing! Tears welled up in her eyes. She could feel her heart pound in her throat. Whatever you do, don't over-react, she told herself. Stay calm. Do *not* panic.

"Samantha! Sean! Sara! Stephen!" Shirley screeched at the top of her lungs. She jumped up and down in her soggy boots, attempting to peer over the heads of the masses. Maybe Samantha had simply found one of her friends and wandered of, leaving the baby unattended. Maybe Sara had been stolen and the rest of the kids were chasing the kidnapper. Maybe Sean had seen a toy he wanted and away. Maybe . . .

She craned her neck and listened for any familiar cry or voice, but the only noise she could hear was the clamor of the Christmas crowd. People packed as tight as festive cotton balls, bobbing red and green, moving in every direction like they were being propelled on electric walkways. No one looked familiar, no one sounded familiar.

Why? Why had she been so foolish as to leave her children by themselves, even for a few brief minutes? She watched *America's Most Wanted*. She knew the risks. Any mall in America was a haven for madmen, kidnappers, and derelicts. And to think she called herself a mother! How many times in the past week had she wished to be free of her clamoring kids—just for five minutes. Now those five minutes were turning into every mother's worst nightmare.

The tears flowed freely as people shuttled by, either staring right at her or making it obvious that they were trying not to. Shirley took a deep breath and prepared to bellow for the police. That's when she heard that welcome teenage whine.

"Mom! You said *you* would change him!" It was Samantha, indignant, but safe and flanked by the other children. "As soon as we got in here, Stephen started to stink up the whole mall, so we went to the bathroom to change his diaper. You owe me one. A *big* one!"

Sara stared up at Shirley from the stroller. "Sean drives too fast. We about ran over an old lady."

"I do *not* drive too fast!" Sean protested. "I missed that old woman by a mile!"

"How come she screamed, then?"

"Maybe she saw your ugly face!"

Sara's little nostrils flared in furry. Shirley felt dizzy, the circulation beginning to return to her head. The nightmare was over.

"Hey, Mom!" Sean yanked at her jacket, "I saw a Monster Mountain Masher in the toy store down at the end of the mall. You know how bad I want a Monster Mountain Masher. It's the only thing I *really* want for Christmas. Can we get one, please! *Pleeeze!*"

Sara kicked at Sean's shins but missed, and nailed Shirley just above the ankle. "I want one, too!"

"You want everything," scolded Samantha. "I deserve a new CD, or maybe a pair of jeans, for rescuing the mall from Stephen's bomb."

"Why—you made *me* throw it away!" Sara wailed. "I deserve something, too!"

Sara cocked her head and stared curiously at her mother. "Are you *crying*, Mommy?"

Shirley wiped the tears from her cheeks and tried to swallow the lump lodged in her throat. Her heart was still pounding, but at least it was in sync with the throbbing in her shin.

Samantha looked alarmed. "Are we late for Nordstrom's half-off salc?"

Shirley shook her head, wiping her nose with one of the baby's wet wipes from the diaper bag. "I'm okay now."

"Then what are we waiting for?" Sean questioned impatiently. "Let's go get my Monster Mountain Masher!"

"No!" Samantha yelped, punching Sean in the shoulder. "We're going to Nordstrom. Mom promised."

Shirley stared at the throngs of people that surrounded them, mulling in every direction. Forget the gliding walkways. The motion of the mall now seemed more like a confused colony of ants, whose hill had just been reconstructed by an unwelcome footstep.

"Come here," she instructed, gathering her children around

her. "I think we had better devise a plan just in case you get lost again."

"But *we* weren't the ones who were lost, Mommy," Sara insisted. "*You* were."

Four

When they arrived at the front entrance to Nordstrom, they discovered that the place had opened two hours earlier for a special before-the-rest-of-the-mall-opens sale. The long tables boasting HALF OFF signs were practically barren. Shirley shrugged and turned the stroller she was pushing around.

"Where are we going?" Samantha asked, blocking her mother's path with the other stroller.

"No use shopping here now. All the sale stuff will be picked over. I didn't realize they opened so early this morning."

Samantha's brow furrowed, her left eye squinted quizzically. "So what if all the sale stuff is gone? All the good stuff is still here. Let's go get some good stuff for a change."

Shirley placed her hand on her daughter's shoulder, gently but firmly. "Sami, I can't afford the good stuff here—just the sale stuff."

"Right," was the only word Samantha managed. Her eyes rolled in disgust, tempting her mother to lose her temper, barge out of the mall, and head for home in a huff.

"Let's go find a Monster Mountain Masher before they're all gone," Sean suggested hopefully.

"Later." Shirley whirled the stroller back down the same way they had come. "First, let's go see Santa."

The troops followed—if not enthusiastically, at least obediently.

The end of the line had to be a mile from the king's red velvet chair where Santa sat perched like a giant doll.

"I'll tell you what." Shirley attempted negotiations with a sulking Samantha and an impatient Sean. "If you'll wait with me in line so Sara and Stephen can have their pictures taken with Santa, we'll do a two-hour whirlwind tour of all your favorite stores."

Samantha actually smiled. Sean made Shirley vow to at least check out the Monster Mountain Mashers.

"No whining?" She pushed for a promise.

"I won't whine if Sami doesn't whine," was the only guarantee she could secure.

The peace treaty expired fifteen minutes later.

"This line hasn't moved two inches!" Samantha complained. "I'm bored."

"I know," said Shirley, attempting to hear the strains of "Have a Holly, Jolly Christmas" above the yammer of the mall.

"A tortoise moves faster," said Sean.

"Let me go shopping around the mall while you wait in line," begged Samantha. "I'll be back by the time the kids get ready to sit on Santa's lap."

Shirley frowned. "No way am I letting you out of my sight again."

"I'm not a child, Mother."

"And I'm not having this argument."

"That's not fair."

Sean was now sitting cross-legged on the ground in front of her. She scooted him forward another inch with her still-soggy boot, while she managed to nudge the strollers forward as well.

"See, we're making progress." She attempted to conjure a smile.

Samantha only scowled.

Shirley leaned over and whispered, "I'm sorry, Sami. It's not my job to be fair. I'm your mother."

Samantha snorted.

Sara tugged at Shirley's coat. "I have to go potty."

"You'll have to wait, honey. If I take you now, we'll lose our place in line."

"I can take her," Samantha suddenly volunteered.

"No, you can't. I told you, we are staying together. This is family fun time, remember?"

Samantha snorted again, this time loud enough to turn heads. "It's not like you're going anywhere for the next two hours."

Shirley shot her a stare that shut Samantha's mouth, buckled her knees, and sent her to the floor next to Sean, who was yawning and nearly asleep.

* * *

Exactly fifty-four minutes later, the winding line had snaked to a head, and Sara was finally astride Santa's velvet knee.

Now that they were up close and personal, Shirley squinted at the jolly old elf in red velour. The bells jingled. The nose was big and round. The costume was vibrant, the beard was shiny synthetic white with shades of curly blue, the hands were gloved and the feet donned big black leather boots. Even the belly shook like a bowl full of jelly. Still . . . she couldn't be sure, but this year's Santa looked an awfully lot like the jolly old cashier at the local Pic 'n' Save store where they shopped practically every weekend.

A *woman* Santa?

Cool.

"Why don't you let Santa hold your little guy?" Santa asked, reaching for Stephen.

"Hey, Santa sounds like the lady at Pic 'n' Save!" shouted Sean, who was now wide awake and staring without pretense.

Shirley handed an apprehensive Stephen across the barrier and into Santa's outstretched arms. He immediately started to squirm.

"I want to have a turn," Sean announced. "How come I can't have a turn on Santa's lap?"

"I thought you said this was stupid, and you didn't want any part of it," a very bored and testy Samantha asserted her frustration.

Sean leaped across the chain barrier and stood by Santa's knee. "I changed my mind."

"I haven't had *my* turn!" Sara began crying. She could barely be heard over Stephen's terrified wails.

"Why don't you pay the ten bucks and have a Polaroid of the three of them taken together?" Samantha suggested between gritted teeth. "This is one of those moments you'll want to remember forever. It'll make a great scrapbook page." Her voice dripped sarcasm.

Before Shirley knew it, a odd-looking elf had taken a ten-dollar bill from her and was now behind a camera shouting, "Everybody look this way and smile!"

Sean was trying to whisper his Christmas list in Santa's ear.

Sara's mouth was wide open, since she was still screaming at Sean.

Stephen was dangerously close to wriggling out of Santa's grasp.

Santa looked a little desperate as he, or *she*, tried to keep the dangling blue-and-white beard from completely being pulled off by the battling children.

"Everybody say *Merry Christmas*!" the mint-green elf ordered.

The kids all shuffled and looked in different directions.

The camera flashed.

The elf quickly propelled Stephen back into his mother's arms, then pulled a Polaroid from the back of the camera.

Sean was now pelting his barrage of orders concerning the deluxe model of Monster Mountain Masher. "The blue one, Santa! Don't forget to bring me the *blue* one!"

Little Sara, however, sat immobile. The look on her face was one of total horror.

Shirley quickly passed Stephen into Samantha's arms and hoisted herself very unladylike over the barrier, knocking down an entire roped section. She didn't care. She scooped a petrified Sara into her arms.

Too late.

Santa's knee was already soaked, the dark stain clearly evident, but not as obvious as the small puddle that now trickled down and all around Santa's shiny black boot.

"It's okay, baby," Shirley whispered reassuringly into Sara's ear, cuddling her head into a bulge of Shirley's jacket. "It was just a little accident. We all have them."

Then Shirley, undaunted, smiled at a distraught Santa and mouthed, "So sorry!"

In her attempt to jockey their way out of there without further delay, Shirley had the presence of mind to grab something from the nearest elf's outstretched hand. She then turned to the 999 people still waiting in line, all staring open-mouthed at Shirley and her stroller brigade. "Merry Christmas, everybody!" she wailed, waving the ten-dollar Polaroid.

Within seconds, Shirley and her children disappeared into welcome obscurity, swallowed by the swirling sea of seasonal shoppers.

Five

Following thirty minutes in the rest room, and after the purchase of a brand new outfit, including shoes and a package of Barney underwear, Sara was sufficiently recovered from her humiliation.

"Can we go shopping *now*?" Samantha wanted to know. "*I'm* the one who deserves a new outfit."

Shirley forced a smile. "Yes, dear. I appreciate your patience."

"Why you don't trust me to go by myself and meet you somewhere later?"

"It's not *you* I don't trust, it's everyone else."

"That's real healthy, Mom."

"When did you turn *thirty*?" Shirley asked, surprised by Samantha's mature blend of humor and cynicism.

"Let's go buy a Monster Mountain Masher before they're all gone," Sean whined, visibly out of patience.

Samantha pointed her finger at her brother's face. "No! You guys promised that Mom and I could shop without your whining for the next two hours. So shut up and let us shop."

"You shut up! I never promised anything!" he shouted back, then glared at Shirley accusingly.

"But I'm hungry," Sara whimpered, "and my new shoes hurt my feet."

"You're in a stroller, so stop whining," Samantha commanded. "I'm the one who's walking, and *I'm* the one who deserves new shoes."

Shirley halted, placed both hands firmly on Samantha's shoulders, and whispered a mother's desperate proposal. "Let's stop by the food court on the way to the department store. I'll buy the kids a burger and then we can shop in peace."

Samantha finally relented, but only after Shirley promised some early Christmas presents.

* * *

The mall's food court was the only place on the planet where all the kids' cravings could be satisfied at once. Samantha ate Chinese, Sean had pizza, and Sara wolfed down a cheeseburger with curly fries. Shirley sampled bites of everything while she fed Stephen from a jar of mashed bananas she had packed in his diaper bag.

By the time they all had feasted on the best cuisine the mall had to offer, and Sara and Stephen were sleeping contentedly in their strollers, and once Samantha was finally appeased with enough packages, Sean was right back in his mother's face.

Shirley winked at him. "Don't worry, sweetheart. The human race is outnumbered by Monster Mountain Mashers—two to one. They are piled to the ceiling in every toy store in the mall. I'm sure Santa's elves will have no problem finding you one for Christmas."

He wasn't convinced. "You understand the blue one is the most powerful one? It's the one that can crush tall buildings. It's got torpedoes on its wheels and missiles on its arms! It's the only one I want. The red one's wimpy."

Shirley ran her hand over the top of her son's buzzed hair, the summer butch cut that still had some growing to do before it would lay flat.

"Don't worry, honey. You've been a great kid all year; I have a feeling Santa will not forget your blue masher thing. Now, help me find something for your father for Christmas."

"He wants a Harley-Davidson," piped Samantha.

Shirley sighed. "A Harley has been at the top of your father's Christmas list for as long as I've known him."

"Then why hasn't he gotten one yet?" Sean asked.

Shirley grinned, teasing, "Maybe your daddy hasn't been such a good boy."

"No way," Samantha rushed to her father's defense. "Dad's name has been on the list at the Harley-Davidson dealer's forever. One of these days they are going to call and tell him his bike is in. He's going to let me ride it."

"In your twisted dreams, Sami!" clamored Sean. "He's going to let *me* ride it!"

Sean swung at Samantha, but Shirley caught his fist in midair. "Enough of that, young man! Now is not the time to pick a fight with your sister. Santa just might be listening."

Sean retreated. "Yeah, right."

Samantha gloated. "Just think of all the boys that will ask me out when they know our family is a *Harley* family."

Shirley's mind abruptly painted a picture of black leather, greasy hair, and glinting switchblades. "I don't want to think about it," she moaned. "We can't get your father a Harley-Davidson this Christmas, but we can get him a new suit."

Samantha and Sean both threw her looks of sheer disgust.

"What?" She feigned surprise. "It's not like his old one still fits. Your dad hasn't been able to button the jacket for years."

More glares.

"Okay," she caved, "how about a fishing pole?"

"Better," said Sean, "but it's not a Harley."

"I want a Harley. I want a fishing pole," murmured Sara, now awake.

The truth was, Shirley knew how much Stan had always wanted a genuine Harley-Davidson. No wanna-be bikes. It had to be the *real* thing. Shiny black. Brand-new. Expensive as a new car. But it was the only material "biggie" that Stan had ever really asked for, and Shirley wished she could buy him one. Three years ago when they had put his name on the local dealer's list, they'd been told the wait might take as long as five years. Something about supply and demand.

"In five years we might be able to afford one," Shirley had said, only half-encouragingly.

Now, three years later, they were no closer to affording such an extravagance, but that didn't stop Stan, a big little boy so much like Sean, from dreaming about his Harley; and it didn't stop Shirley from dreaming about making her husband happy. Someday. Someday she would address her own wish list, too.

There wasn't much Shirley would not do to make her family happy. She had once read that the *lack* of money was the root of all evil. The thought made her smile, and she wondered if the warm feeling coursing through her body was the Visa card smoldering from excess use.

By early afternoon all the "good stuff" had either been bought or destroyed by festive shoppers. Shirley felt beat, and now keenly aware what a stupid idea it had been to have her children accompany her Christmas shopping.

Not one item she'd purchased so far was on her list, nor had it been on sale. She had blown a good share of her Christmas budget, and had nothing except one long red box to put under the tree. That "good tidings" feeling was fading fast, and now there was no doubt that the rising temperature was caused by the melting plastic in her purse.

"I get to tell Daddy about his fishing pole as soon as we get home!" Sara announced.

"No! I get to!" Sean had been unable to say much all day without feeling the need to scream it at the top of his lungs.

Samantha put a finger to her lips. "It's supposed to be a secret."

"Yes, kids," Shirley groaned. "Please don't say a word to Daddy. He'll be so surprised on Christmas morning." She knew there was no hoping that the secret could be kept long enough to surprise anyone.

"I'm hungry," Sara announced for the twentieth time that day.

"But you just ate a whole cheeseburger and fries," her mother reminded her.

"Now I want vanilla ice cream with sprinkles."

"It's the middle of winter . . ." Shirley started to reason, but lacked the strength.

They found an ice-cream shop with a line of shivering people waiting for double-scoops of their favorite flavors. Shirley was holding a fussy and squirming Stephen, assuring him that this day would really not last forever—it only *felt* like it would. The young girl behind the ice-cream counter suddenly smiled, bright and cheerful.

Shirley could not help returning the smile. It made her feel good. After all, this was the season of goodwill toward everyone. Besides, the pointed Santa hat on top of the girl's head bonged back and forth as she swayed to the buzz of the mall's holiday music. Her enthusiasm was clearly contagious. She reached across the counter and handed Shirley a vanilla cone with loads of chocolate sprinkles.

Shirley smiled again, passing the cone to Sara and giving the girl a five-dollar bill.

"That's sure a cute baby you've got there," she squeaked, sounding exactly like Shirley imagined a real elf might.

"Thanks. Keep the change," Shirley offered, an unexpected surge of generosity sweeping through her.

"Thanks, lady," squeaked the girl. "You must be a very proud grandma."

It took a while for the comment to register. When it did, Shirley turned away, flushed with a feeling that was anything but generous or festive.

"We've leaving *now*." The way she barked it made the children realize there was no use in arguing, except for Sean, who stood in front of his mother, blocking the stroller.

"Please, please, buy me a blue Monster Mountain Masher before we go," he begged.

Her eyes flamed.

He stepped out of the way to let his mother blow past toward the nearest exit.

It was Shirley's best feat all day.

They trudged across the parking lot through small mountains of black slush. Shirley had to fold up both strollers and carry them, forcing Sara to walk and Sami to lug Stephen. Sean was laden down with packages, none of them his Monster Mountain Masher.

By the time they reached the car, everyone was wet, half frozen, and worn to the core.

"I'm still hungry," Sara sniffled. They were the only words anyone spoke all the way home.

When they walked through the front door, Stan was watching television and a blazing fire was roaring in the family room.

"I know what you're getting for Christmas!" Sara broadcast to her father the minute they were inside.

Shirley shook her head avidly. "Shhhh"

"Yeah, Sara," threatened Sean. "Dad's fishing pole is supposed to be a surprise, remember?"

Stan played along, pretending he did not to hear the unintended proclamation. He simply looked at Shirley and winked. "I got finished at work early, and I think I've actually caught that 'Ho, ho, ho' sprit. What do you say we take a family excursion to the mall?"

Shirley instantly felt very old. "Ho, ho, ho," she said, in her best *grandmotherly* voice.

Six

It took Shirley the rest of the day to recover from her great mall adventure, but by Saturday morning she was back to her jolly "old" self.

She sang the first lines from "White Christmas" as she poured milk on Sara's corn flakes.

"What's a white Christmas?" Sara asked.

Shirley smiled. "It's a snowy one."

"But snow's not white," Sara protested, crunching a mouthful of flakes. "It's kind of icky gray."

"That's just because of the pollution," Samantha leaned across the table to explain. "Snow's not supposed to be gray."

"Yeah," Sean agreed. "It didn't used to be, did it?" He turned toward Shirley, mopping a small puddle of spilled milk with his elbow. "*Before* the olden days, when you were a girl, snow was pure white, wasn't it, Mom?"

"Excuse me," growled Shirley, still stinging from yesterday's "grandmother" episode. "Did you just say that I was born *before* the olden days?"

Stan entered just in time to catch the question. "Don't go there, kids. Haven't you learned that there are two things you never mention about a woman? First, never bring up her age, except to say how young she looks. And never, ever mention her weight."

"Not even to say how skinny she looks?" Sean wanted to know.

"No, son. Trust me, just don't ever bring up a woman's weight. Your life will run a lot smoother."

Shirley spread an onion bagel with cream cheese and sat it before Stan. "When did you become the resident sage? Your sensitivity and insight astound me." She was only teasing, and he knew it.

"Just call me Solomon," he rejoined. "What would you like to do today to celebrate the season?"

"I'd like to stand around all day and watch you string up the Christmas lights on the outside of the house."

His eyes darted toward the children. "Hey, kids, what do you say we go downtown and pick out the biggest Christmas tree we can find?"

The cheers went up from the troops. Even baby Stephen gooed his support. Shirley knew she was defeated, but not deflated. Theirs would have to survive another year, as the only house on the block that remained dark during the entire season of light. Oh well, she still had that ratty Rudolph wreath she could hang on the door. At least his nose glowed a red welcome to festive well-wishers.

Stan drove around town for 45 minutes in bumper-to-bumper traffic before they located a Christmas tree lot. It was nearly as crowded as the mall had been, but there were plenty of trees—a virtual forest had been chopped to the ground just for this occasion.

The minute they were out of the car, Stan and the children dashed off toward the tallest, bushiest trees on the lot. Shirley just stood immobile, taking in the sawed-off forest.

"Do you have *living* trees?" she asked the first person she saw, a young man dressed smartly either as a warm employee or a rapper. He was wearing a dark overcoat, knit cap, and gloves with the fingers cut out.

He was a rapper. "I don't work here, lady. What do I look like, a Christmas tree salesman?"

"It's hard to tell beneath all of those layers," she muttered, blowing a puff of warm air into her cupped hands. She hadn't realized how cold it was until that moment. The next person she suspected might be an employee was donning a bright red Santa cap atop his head and a Christmas tree embroidered onto the back on his jean jacket. "Do you work here?" she asked.

"What, don't I look like a Christmas tree salesman?" he snarled.

Shirley smiled. "Do you sell living trees?"

He thrust a thumb into the air. "In the back corner."

Then he was gone.

Shirley beckoned the rest of the family over to her. "Let's choose a tree together," she suggested.

Stan had Stephen snuggled warmly inside his coat, reminding Shirley of a kangaroo pouch. "I thought that's what we were doing," he said.

"Yeah, we want a tree that's taller than our house," Sean announced.

As it turned out, everyone had an opinion about selecting the family Christmas tree.

"I like this fat tree."

"No, this tall skinny one is the one I want."

"How come we can't get this one? It's perfect."

Shirley inspected the perfect tree that had caught Samantha's attention. "Honey, we don't want that tree."

"Why not, Mom? What's wrong with it?"

"Look closely. It's fake."

"Yeah," chuckled the salesman, whose hat reminded Shirley of the ice-cream server at the mall, the one who had deemed her a grandmother. "Everybody wants to buy our artificial tree."

Stan frowned. "Why do you have an artificial tree in the middle of all of these live trees?"

The salesman's chuckle exploded into an unnerving laugh. "Ain't none of these trees live, mister. I put it there to prove a point—that society prefers plastic perfection to flawed reality."

Shirley knew that the man was making a statement; at another time, in another place that wasn't so cold, she might have stayed to discuss society's downfall with him. Instead, she kept walking toward the back corner of the lot where there were a dozen or so pine trees planted in small pots. The tallest tree was three feet high. *Maybe*. Nearly all of the trees were scraggly and forlorn.

"Charlie Brown trees!" declared Samantha. "I think we should get this one." She grabbed a pot with one lone brownish branch protruding upward.

"I was hoping they'd be bigger and a little fuller," Shirley admitted, trying not to sound disappointed.

Stan whistled. "Have you seen the price tags? These sorry little things cost twice as much as those towers in the middle of the lot."

Shirley was aware that Stan did not share her vision and new interest in saving the environment one living tree at a time, but she was determined to stick to her guns. "I would really like a living tree this year."

He shrugged and gave her one of his signature patronizing glowers. "Why? It'll be like all your houseplants—dead by New Year's."

She reached over and flipped him with the end of Stephen's dangling scarf. "If you think those little barbs don't hurt, they do. So what if I'm not Ewell Gibbons?"

Stan shot her a blank stare.

"Forget it. Just forget it. I don't ask for much, Stan. Lights strung around the outside of the house, a Christmas tree that hasn't been axed to death. That's it. Allow me one out of two."

He chuckled.

"Don't you dare laugh at me!" Her tone sounded harsher than she felt. The tree wasn't a monumental issue in her life, just a little one. Maybe it was the little things that set her off. A few people were beginning to stop and stare. Shirley didn't care. She read the tag on the tallest of the living trees.

"A hearty blue spruce is not exactly a delicate African violet that needs precisely the right amount of sunlight and water," sneered Shirley. " All I have to do to this tree is water it and then plant it in the yard once Christmas is over."

Stan rubbed his hands together and blew a steam cloud against his red knuckles. "In case you haven't noticed, it's freezing out here and the ground is as hard as granite. You're not going to be able to dig a hole until it thaws in the spring. What are you going to do with your tree until then?"

The children had been patiently listening to their parents bicker, but now that they had been reminded of the frigid temperature, they began complaining.

"I'm cold, Daddy," said Sara. "Please let Mommy get the tree so we can have Christmas all year long!"

"I can put it in my room," Sean volunteered.

"Yeah, yeah," Samantha taunted. "There's enough dirt on your bedroom floor to plant a whole forest."

Sean swung at her, but Samantha was keen to backing away, just in time. "Shut up, Sam!"

"Don't call me Sam. Call me Samantha or Sami, but not Sam."

"Sam! Sam! Sam! You look like an ugly old man!"

This time it was Samantha who swung at Sean. She clipped him on the bottom of the chin. He looked more shocked than hurt.

Stan yanked at his coat's zipper, then thrust Stephen at Shirley, who was trying to separate her two eldest children from a genuine brawl.

"Stop it this instant! Both of you!" she wailed.

Their brawl was attracting a curious crowd. Even the surly tree salesman was gawking in their direction.

Stan stepped between Samantha and Sean. "Knock it off!" he reprimanded. "This is supposed to be a fun family time. Now shut up and have fun!"

The irony of the moment was not lost on Shirley, and she burst out laughing. The scuffle was over.

"Let's just get a flocked pinion pine like we do every year," suggested Stan.

"I don't want a flocked tree this year," Shirley stood her ground. "There's something *phony* about a flocked tree."

"Duh," said Sean. "The snow's not real, Mom."

"I know that," Shirley huffed. "That's my point. A flocked tree is as phony as that plastic one Samantha almost fell for. Fake. Artificial. It's symbolic of all that's gone wrong with this season."

"Oh brother, *Mother*," Samantha stepped in as mediator. "Why don't you get your living tree and put it in the front room, and let Daddy get his flocked tree and put it in the family room?"

Stan and Shirley stared at their sage teenager. Samantha had always been wise beyond her years, and both her parents were learning more and more to appreciate her common sense and calming influence.

"Cool!" said Sami. "Two trees! Twice as many presents!"

Decorating two trees turned out to be a lot of fun, worth the extra work. Shirley popped a giant tub of buttered popcorn and made hot cocoa with tiny marshmallows. She put on a CD of the season's best, then dropped two more cinnamon sticks into her crockpot.

She paraphrased the famous song by noting that it was beginning to smell a lot like Christmas, as the kids argued over the Christmas stockings.

Stan lugged a half dozen boxes labeled "Christmas Decorations" down from the attic. Most of the boxes were packed with hopelessly tangled and wadded strands of Christmas lights. After half an hour of wrestling with the same strand, Stan gave up and tossed them in the kitchen garbage can.

"I don't understand why you can't roll these up straight when you pack them," he scolded Shirley. "Every year we go through this same nonsense."

Shirley wasn't going to let Stan's sudden bout of orneriness chase away the spirit she was enjoying. "You know, sweetheart, every year when *I* take down the tree and box the lights and decorations, *I* make sure everything is in perfect order. The bulbs are all whole and shiny. The lights in exact order. No knots. No tangles. But every holiday when we open up those boxes, some of the ornaments are broken and the lights are always tangled. I swear there must be a conspiracy. I suspect it's the same troublemakers who hide in the clothes dryer and steal one sock every time I put in a matching pair."

Stan didn't exactly grin, but he came close enough. Shirley wished she could always dissipate tension with humor, but avoiding arguments usually took more effort than actually arguing. Today however, was worth the expended energy.

Soon the lights were twinkling around both trees, allowing Stan and Shirley the luxury of more or less lying back on the sofa, observing as Samantha, Sean and Sara decorated.

The small living tree got the royal "Charlie Brown" treatment. Its branches were covered with all of the homemade ornaments.

"My mother never allowed me to display my handcrafted decorations," Shirley reflected, "because they didn't match her precise theme for the year. To be honest, I'll bet Lena just threw all my paper angels, macaroni reindeer and marshmallow Santas away."

"Well, I'm glad you're not your mother," said Stan, handing her Sean's kindergarten wise man made from ancient Play-Doh.

"Me, too."

Shirley's favorite ornaments were the ones the kids had created over the years. Stan's favorites were the ones engraved "Baby's First Christmas" with the names and years that each child was born. This year Stan surprised everyone with a silver rattle engraved "Baby's First Christmas" followed by Stephen's name and birth date.

"When on earth did you find time to shop for that?" She was clearly touched by her husband's sentimentality.

"I ordered it from Hallmark before you even came home from the hospital with Stephen."

She had to bite her bottom lip to keep from saying, "Oh, you had time to order a Christmas ornament for the baby, but *I* had to order my own flowers!" Shirley managed to keep silent and just squeezed Stan's hand.

"Ouch!" he yipped. "Not so hard!"

The tall traditional tree got the commercial treatment. Red and green satin balls and gold bows. The twinkling lights bathed branches and bulbs in a warm glow.

"It's beautiful," Samantha pronounced. "Even Grandma Lena would like this one."

"Don't bet on it," Shirley muttered.

Sara was pulling on Stan's shirttail. "Don't forget that I get to put the angel on top this year. Daddy, you promised."

Stan hoisted her to his shoulders while everyone shouted directions, until Sara had placed a small crystal angel on the very tip-top branch of the pinion pine.

The angel was the first ornament Shirley and Stan had bought after they were married. The first year it was the *only* ornament on their tree—a tree that was truly worthy of Charlie Brown. It was so small and scraggly that the man at the lot had taken pity on the tree and the young newlyweds, and had given it to them for free.

That was one of the happiest Christmases Shirley had ever known.

The rest of the day was spent setting up the creche, hanging the well-worn wreath on the front door, stationing silk poinsettias around the rooms, and adding all of the festive touches that transformed their everyday house into a very special holiday home.

Shirley requested that everyone help clean up any messes. The best part of her day was when they all cooperated without any further bickering. After the vacuum was put away, Shirley stood back, surveyed her decorated domain, and let the spirit of the holiday sweep over her.

"What do you think?" asked Stan.

"I think it would never pass Martha Stewart's white glove test."

"Who's Martha Stewart, and why do you care what she thinks? I was hoping to spend the rest of the day as a family. You haven't invited Martha over, have you?"

Shirley cracked a smile. "Forget Martha. You know you still have time to hang those lights on the outside of the house. Just think of that great big box of outdoor lights that have never even been tangled because they've never been used."

Shirley realized she was walking a fine line between whining and manipulation. Stan simply refused to walk it with her. He was halfway down the hallway before Shirley finished.

"What's for dinner?" he called back.

"Turkey casserole."

"Turkey?" Sean suddenly appeared. "Roasted turkey. Turkey enchiladas. Turkey soup. Even turkey omelettes, and now turkey casserole. I'm sick of turkey."

Little Sara, popping out from behind him, chimed, "Me, too!"

Stan made a U-turn. "What do you say I take the whole family out to dinner tonight at your mom's favorite restaurant?"

Shirley put her arm around her husband's waist and whispered in his ear, "I say that was my 'turkey plan' all along."

Seven

The fleeting miracles of Christmas, those flashing moments that warmed Shirley's heart, filling it with genuine good cheer, were moments she intended to focus on this season. She was determined to capture the spirit and lock it away like a child capturing a butterfly, securing it in a glass jar with holes poked through the lid, allowing the creature breath, but not freedom.

"Shirley, you're full of it," Stan joked when she caught him underneath the plastic mistletoe she had hung from their bedroom ceiling with an enormous silver thumbtack. "Don't you realize that the Christmas spirit is not something anyone can *capture*? No matter how much money you spend or how good your decorations look or how festive the house smells—"

"Oh, I am just in a happy mood. Come on over here and let me show you some good tidings!"

"Wish I could, but I can't be late for work this morning. I'm facing a crazy few weeks trying to get a proposal written for a contract from New Delhi, India. Curtis has assigned me detail duty."

"That Scrooge."

"Which reminds me," said Stan, wiping a dab of leftover shaving cream from his jawline, "don't forget about the company Christmas party."

"When is it?"

"I forget, but I will call and tell you. I know you're supposed to coordinate with the other wives on a planning committee."

"Me? Why me? I don't understand why your dinky company still thinks these are the fifties. Housewives with our only mission—to serve our working husbands and make them happy."

Stan grimaced. "Watch it, babe—your happy mood is in flames. Besides, I'm not any happier about this company party than you are."

"Maybe you just mask it better," she offered, wondering

why her emotions were so insane lately. One minute she was ecstatic, the next down in the dumps. Stephen was six months old, too old for her to be able to claim she was still suffering from "the baby blues."

"Where is all this hostility coming from?" Stan asked.

All Shirley could do was shrug. "I guess Christmas with a crazy woman doesn't sound too fun, does it?"

He looked into the mirror and straightened his tie. "Don't worry, we're used to it."

She hoped he was joking. "Why doesn't Curtis just unzip his wallet and spring for a real caterer?"

Stan brushed his lips across Shirley's forehead.

"Don't patronize me!" she snapped.

"I wasn't. I was just thinking about what you said. I know the company is small, but there aren't very many women who work there. Curtis seems to prefer men."

"Chauvinist pig. Too cheap for a caterer for the company Christmas party!"

"Shirley, you've forgotten back when the company used to hire professional caterers. Remember when we went as couples to real swanky restaurants? You are the one who griped because the parties were not family oriented enough. You're the one who made all of the fuss. You're the one—"

"Okay, okay. Just call me when you know the date and time. I don't want it to conflict with any of our other holiday plans."

Stan splashed cologne on his face. "What other holiday plans?"

"Well, I want to have a couple of holiday parties of our own. One for the kids and maybe a potluck buffet with a few of our friends."

He grimaced. "What friends?"

Shirley realized he had her there. It was true that both Stan and Shirley had a great many acquaintances, but when it came right down to it, friends were scarce. For better or worse, they were each other's best friends.

"We're pathetic, aren't we?" she teased.

"*We*?" he gibed back.

Then Shirley thought of Rita. "Have you found an eligible man from your office to line Rita up with yet?"

"How do you know Rita *wants* to be lined up? Has she even told you the story behind her two divorces?"

"Not really," Shirley had to admit. "But I know she works all the time and I never hear anything about a social life. She's a wonderful woman with so much to offer."

"And you think she has to offer it to a man?"

Shirley fell back onto the bed that she had just made. "Forget it. I'll find the perfect match for her."

"Sure you will, Shirl. Sure you will. But keep in mind that the perfect man has already been taken—by you!" He tossed a pillow at her and was gone.

Shirley crawled back between the sheets and told her body to relax, to enjoy the rare moments of such a quiet morning. She had barely adjusted her pillow in the perfect position when Sean burst through the door.

"Dad said I could go play at Collin's house," he announced, loud enough to wake Stephen, who was in a cradle next to the master bed.

"Have you eaten breakfast yet?" Shirley asked.

"No, but Collin's mom will feed me. She makes awesome French toast."

Collin was Sean's new friend from across the street. "How do you know what kind of French toast his mother makes?"

"Remember, I ate there yesterday morning."

Stephen began to stretch and whimper. She lifted him and placed him next to her underneath the covers. "Why don't you lie here and snuggle with us for a while, then I'll get up and make you French toast with hot maple syrup?" she tried to coax Sean.

"I'm not sleepy."

She pulled back a corner of the comforter and patted the mattress. Sean jumped aboard, bouncing them all into the air.

"How come baby Stephen hardly ever cries?" asked Sean.

Shirley felt her body immediately tense. "I guess he's just a very good-natured baby," she replied, although she had some deeply suppressed concerns of her own about why Stephen was so "good-natured" and quiet.

"I mean, why does he just lie there most of the time? He hardly ever kicks or moves around, and he doesn't make very many baby noises."

"He cries," she said defensively.

"Not very much. Collin's baby sister cries all the time. She kicks, screams, and even laughs out loud."

"So what? Stephen is just a little slower than some babies, that's all." Shirley refused to address the concerns she might be harboring about Stephen. Not now. Not this morning. No. Right now she just wanted to lie there with both of her sons cuddled in her arms. They were *both* perfect. Just perfect.

They would have all been back asleep in a few more minutes if the phone didn't ring.

Sean grabbed it. "It's for Sami," he announced. Then he blared at the top of his lungs, only three inches away from his mother's ear, "Sami, it's for you!"

Samantha bounded in, bouncing them all once more into the air. Stephen didn't laugh, but he didn't cry either.

"Who wants to talk to me?" Samantha asked, then quickly added, "If it's Grandma asking me to help with her housework, tell her I have a sore throat."

"It's not Grandma," said Sean.

"Then who is it and what do they want?"

"Who are you and what do you want?" Sean repeated the query into the receiver.

"You little idiot!" Samantha steamed.

Sean held out the receiver. "It's a guy."

Samantha grabbed the telephone from her brother. "Hello," she chirped cheerfully.

"So much for the sore throat." Shirley chuckled, then tried to listen nonchalantly while making room for a sleepy Sara, who had just wandered in.

"Really?" Samantha squealed. "Me? Wow! That's great. I'll be there."

"Did you win the lotto?" quizzed Shirley as soon Samantha had hung up.

"No. I'm in!" she shouted.

"In what?" everyone asked her at once.

"In *The Nutcracker*! The lead, Lisa, just broke her ankle, and I'm up for the next Sugarplum Fairy. Isn't it awesome?"

Shirley smiled, but rested there just as mellow as Stephen. She didn't want to spoil Samantha's joy, but she knew immediately what this news would mean to her own holiday schedule. The rehearsal hall was at least a thirty-minute drive—one way. The car would need new tires by the time Christmas arrived. So what—it was already whirling on four baldies.

She let the kids all celebrate the news before she ventured to ask, "How often do you have to rehearse?"

"Every day. I told them I'd be there to meet the rest of the cast and get started this morning by nine-thirty. Is that okay?"

"Of course." Shirley forced herself to sit up. She put her arms around her daughter. "Congratulations, angel. You'll be wonderful."

"Thanks, Mom. Do you know where my ballet bag is?"

While Sean and his siblings were wolfing down French toast, Shirley was reviewing some of the lists she'd made.

First was the gift list. Stan's name topped it, and "Harley-Davidson" was written next to it. Of course, so was fishing pole. Next to Sean's name was written "Monster Mountain Masher. Blue." Samantha was getting more clothes and makeup, something she never had enough of. Sara would be happy with "one of everything." She really wanted a doll that sucked its thumb. Stephen was easy—diapers were all he really needed. She might buy him some of those developmental toys designed to stimulate babies' mental and motor skills. Not that Stephen needed them—no, that wasn't it at all.

The rest of the list consisted of other family members and a few select friends. The card list grew longer every year. One of Shirley's very favorite parts of the holiday season was receiving Christmas cards and letters from people she cared for but only heard from annually. She especially loved the cards that included photos. It was fun to see how people changed from year to year. Even the cheesy "brag" letters were something she looked forward to receiving.

Shirley knew she was procrastinating taking her own family's annual Christmas-card shot. She'd thought about it a few times, but just kept hoping all the pounds she'd gained from Thanksgiving (Thanksgiving*s* over the years) would somehow melt away, before she was forced to smile in front of a camera. That was one chore that could wait, at least for a few more days.

This year Shirley had compiled something new: a *service* list. It was actually something she had always done, but never prioritized like this year. That was due in large part to Rita. Shirley had learned so much from Rita over the past months. She had taken Shirley to heights and depths that she, in her self-revolving world, had never experienced.

Shirley's first official service project for the season was a stop at the battered women's shelter, a place Rita had first introduced her to months ago.

How was Shirley ever going to repay Rita for the dimensions that she had added to her life? She'd think of *something*. . . .

Most of the service projects had to be done in secret to truly be acts of Christian service, but there were others that had to be done out in the open, and needed to be started right away. There was one particularly pressing one that she didn't intend to procrastinate on.

After Shirley dropped Samantha off at *The Nutcracker* rehearsal, she and the other kids headed back to the Christmas tree lot where Shirley bought two more living trees. They weren't quite as big as the one they'd purchased for the family, small enough so that if she turned them sideways, they fit into the van.

Next was a lengthy stop at the grocery store. Shirley divided certain items into certain bags and then drove straight to the women's shelter.

"Thought you could use a little holiday cheer," said Shirley, dragging a tree through the front door. Sean and Sara followed right behind, lugging bulging grocery bags.

Pat, the shelter's director, ran to rescue baby Stephen from under the pinch of his mother's arm.

"Merry Christmas!" she greeted Shirley and kids. "Come on in."

"We can't stay," said Shirley, "but thought this place could use a few early presents."

Sara dropped the sack she was holding. "Mama bought shampoo and makeup for the hurt women."

"And diapers and toys for the kids," Sean added, setting his sack down on the floor.

Pat put her arm around Shirley. "Girl, you know just what this place needs. It's so wonderful to see you bring your healthy, happy kids here. You're teaching them what life is all about—*giving* instead of just getting."

"They are good kids." Shirley shrugged off the compliment. "In fact, we better head out, because Sami's in the local production of *The Nutcracker*."

Sean and Sara took turns hugging Pat and then left with their mother.

* * *

Shirley then raced back to the rehearsal hall just in time to pick up a happy but exhausted Samantha.

"I need to be back tomorrow morning an hour earlier for my costume fitting," she told her mother. "And I need money for costumes."

Shirley sighed. In spite of her careful planning, this was going to be another Christmas than ran on credit.

Shirley fixed a late lunch and left the kids in Samantha's care. "You know how to reach me if you need me. Call nine-one-one if anything happens. I mean anything like a catastrophe."

"Don't worry, Mom. The baby's sound asleep. Sara and Sean are watching a video. I'll keep the doors locked. I can handle it for an hour."

"Sorry, babe. I just worry. Stay off the phone and call Dad at his office if you need him."

"Just go!" Samantha ushered her mother out the door.

Shirley drove across town to a new high-rise condo on the waterfront. The valet, dressed in a green velvet vest, helped her take out the tree and a huge honey-baked ham tied with red and gold ribbons.

"Looks like you're helping Santa out." He smiled, assisting her all the way to the elevator.

"I'm taking these to my friend Rita on the top floor. I called a little while ago, she's expecting me."

"No problem. If you'll give me your keys, I'll park your minivan around back and you can get it when you finish your visit."

Shirley thanked him and handed the man her key ring. For one fleeting minute she looked at him and wondered if she'd just handed her keys to a car-jacker.

He handed her a claim check.

"Thanks," Shirley said, feeling guilty for suspecting him, for being so suspicious of society in general. The vest alone should have assured her that he was legitimate.

Why do you judge people so quickly? she chastised herself. "*Mis*judge is more like it," she muttered, tugging the tree onto the elevator. When she reached the top floor, Shirley got off into a stunning foyer. White plush carpets, black-and-white marbled floors and walls, and polished silver railings. She faced a spectacular view of the glistening waterfront. Shirley was impressed, maybe even a little envious. This was a stark reminder that Rita's world revolved in a very different orbit than her own.

Shirley pulled the tree down the hallway, hoping no one noticed the trail of dirt and needles it was leaving behind. She hoisted the ham underneath her arm, pushing the glowing doorbell next to Rita's apartment number.

The heavy wooden door swung open quickly, and there stood an ever-pressed Rita, dressed in a starched cream linen suit and matching crocheted flats. Hair and makeup flawless, as always. Shirley always felt frumpy around Rita, but not because of anything Rita did, only because of what she was: *picture perfect*.

"Welcome. Come on in," greeted Rita, waving Shirley into her apartment.

Shirley smiled. "Merry Christmas!" She beamed, tugging at the tree, trying to balance the gift ham. The pronounced look of surprise on Rita's face stopped her in her muddy tracks.

"I . . . I know I'm early," Shirley stammered, "but I realize this has been a difficult year for you. I just wanted to make sure you have your best Christmas ever." She set the tree upright and thrust the golden-bowed gift of pork toward her friend.

Rita did not move. Did not speak. Did not blink. Did not remove the look of angst from her expression.

"What's *wrong*?" Shirley questioned slowly.

Rita's ruby lips slowly curled upward. "I . . . I . . . I guess it never came up in our conversations, but, Shirley, you must know—I'm Jewish!"

Eight

The next few seconds clomped through eternity, slow and awkward. They may have hung in the air forever, if Shirley did not do what Shirley always did when she found herself humiliated. She laughed—but only at herself. It started as an embarrassed chuckle, but quickly turned into a hearty belly-laugh. Finally, the humor of her faux pas struck with full force, nearly doubling her over.

"I don't know what to say. Should I apologize? Should I get the Christmas tree out of here? Maybe I could give it to your doorman or the valet. Oh, no! Isn't there a rule that Jewish hands are forbidden to touch pork?" She posed the last concern while snatching the ham away from Rita.

Rita smiled and swung the front door closed. "Don't worry about it; I'm very touched by your thoughtfulness. Though I must admit, this is a first for me." She led Shirley into the kitchen and motioned to the counter where Shirley sat the ham, then wiped the tears of laughter from her cheeks.

"I apologize in every way there is to apologize. I guess my intuitive powers failed me. I should have known you weren't Christian."

Rita raised an arched and perfectly-penciled eyebrow. "I beg your pardon?"

"You don't act like a Christian."

Now Rita's brow furrowed and her narrow shoulders hunched like a linebacker. "You had better clarify that. How *does* a Christian *act*?"

"I didn't mean to offend you." Shirley sensed she was headed into troubled waters, so she quickly did a 180. "Actually, you *do* act like a Christian, Rita. You're loving. Kind. Thoughtful. Honest. And you're always serving others."

Rita barely smiled, but did stand taller.

Shirley should have stopped there, but stopping at the most

appropriate place was never one of Shirley's strong suits. "It's just that most Christians are vocal about their beliefs. We're out to convert the nonbelieving world."

"Oh, really? Well, I've never been one to push my faith on anyone. I think quietly *living* what a person believes is the best form of teaching it." There was an air of authority, but not superiority, in her tone.

"*Teaching versus preaching*. That's a great sermon talk. I'll have to tell my pastor." Her feeble attempt at humor went unacknowledged. For the first time in their budding friendship, Shirley felt tense. Really uneasy. She had never seen Rita bristle like this, not even when the subject of Rita's divorces came up. If they managed to get through this, Shirley vowed to remember that religion was off limits.

Rita opened her refrigerator and poured two glasses of chilled cranberry juice from a large pitcher. She handed one to Shirley and took a sip from the other one.

"Don't be so hard on yourself, Shirley. Now that I think about it, the subject of my faith has never come up in our conversations. If it had, I probably would have told you that I've recently discovered a weakness in my personal conviction. If I seem a little too defensive, it's because of my own doubts, and it has nothing to do with you."

"Well, I'm sorry anyway. I didn't mean to imply that Christians are the only ones who can be loving, kind, thoughtful, honest, and all that jazz. It's just that we're supposed to practice the golden rule. You know, that one that *you* live by so well."

The two women sat on tall silver barstools scalloping Rita's pristine kitchen counter, sipping cranberry juice in relative, but no longer uncomfortable, silence.

Shirley could not contain her quiet demeanor or curiosity for more than a few minutes. "I am just now realizing that I know virtually nothing about Judaism. I confess, I don't even know what Hanukkah is all about."

Rita was recognizably reluctant to talk about her faith, and Shirley sensed she did so more out of obligation than desire. "Jews recognize that much of our time has to be spent in the pursuit of our basic needs, like eating, sleeping, and shopping the best sales."

Shirley didn't know whether to laugh or not. A thin smile was all she ventured.

"That's why God set aside certain holy times," Rita continued, "when we can concentrate on returning to goodness and seeking forgiveness."

"You sound like a rabbi, Rita. I don't understand why you think there is a weakness in your faith."

"Trust me—there is. What you have to understand about Judaism is the distinctions among Orthodox Jews, Conservative Jews, and Reform or Liberal Jews."

Shirley didn't pretend to know what Rita was talking about, but she instinctively related what Rita was saying to herself, and wondered if there was such a thing as "Reform Christians." If not, Shirley suddenly categorized herself as a "Liberal Christian"—one who could pick and choose which doctrines to embrace and which to extinguish. Was there a smorgasbord of Christian beliefs? The idea made Shirley almost queasy, and she abruptly returned her attention to what Rita was saying, something about her grandfather being more Orthodox, but how she considered herself more of a Reform Jew.

"Isn't Hanukkah a lot like Christmas?" Shirley asked, not meaning to shift Rita's direction. "I've always been fascinated by the tradition, the candles, the family unity."

Rita sighed, pushing the air through clenched teeth. "In some ways, I suppose Hanukkah and Christmas are alike. Hanukkah is a time to remember the dedication of our people, and to rebuild our own faith. It's also a time to gather family and loved ones around us to share our high holy time. Unlike Christmas day, it's a week-long festival to commemorate our heritage."

Shirley cocked her head, not sure she was following.

"I'm afraid I'm not much of a storyteller. You know the tale of how a small group of Jewish people waged a battle against their enemies, who were trying to force Jews to abandon their own beliefs and customs. That small band of Jews fought and won so that we can observe our own holidays and rituals as a people."

Shirley could not help silently planning a trip to the library. She wanted to know more about the Jewish faith, to understand the details of what Rita was saying, but she did not want to ask the wrong questions, expose the extent of her ignorance. She had already proven herself an idiot. Shirley thought it was interesting how Rita sometimes referred to Judaism as "us" and "we," but sometimes "they" and "them."

Shirley realized she had to choose her words wisely—broadly. "It sounds like Hanukkah is a very special time for you."

Rita frowned. "It is supposed to be."

"When is Hanukkah, anyway?"

"It starts next week."

"Are you going to celebrate it?"

"I think my menorah is still packed away in a box somewhere around here." Rita turned to rinse her glass at the sink.

"I have an idea," Shirley piped. "I hope it won't be offensive, so tell me if I'm way off base, but do you have anything against Christmas?"

Rita pivoted and gazed at Shirley.

"I know you don't believe in Jesus Christ," Shirley said quickly, "but is there a rule that says you *can't* celebrate Christmas with your Christian friends?"

"Depends who you're talking to," answered Rita deliberately. "That's part of my problem. Jews are nearly as diversified as Christians in their theology. Every rabbi I've talked to in my adult life has a different take on how things should be done—what's acceptable and what's not.

"I suppose if a Jew has a clear sense of her own religious identity, it would be all right to participate at a Christmas event. I have never really done that. I mean, I've gone to Christmas parties and such, but never actually celebrated. I guess I thought it would make me a hypocrite or something."

"I don't think it would."

"I used to envy my Christian friends when I was a child," Rita reflected. "They got the presents, the parties, the shiny paper, and flickering lights. I got a lecture about my Jewish heritage. But not all Jews are like that. I suppose it just depends on your personal circumstances."

Shirley was a bit confused. "What about *you*?"

"Oh, I don't know if I would miss a good party, given the chance, but my basic belief is this: Christmas is a *Christian* holiday. For non-Christians like me, it's a festive time of parties and decorations. For you, it's the most sacred holiday of the year. Your highest holy day. It commemorates the birth of Jesus Christ—*your* savior."

Shirley fell silent, suddenly finding it hard to swallow. Which term was it that now lodged in her throat—highest holy day or savior? Maybe both.

"Besides," Rita continued, "Jews have more than enough holidays of their own without having to borrow any from you Christians."

Now it was Rita's attempt at humor that went unacknowledged. Shirley's mind was flooded with what Rita had said. Christmas *should* be treated as the highest holy day, the birthdate of Jesus Christ. For people who called themselves Christians, people like Shirley, the holiday should be looked forward to and commemorated with a rededication of faith. At that moment, just thinking about all of the trimmings and trappings of the season, and the madness of the mall, seemed absurd.

Shirley was quiet for an uncharacteristically long stretch.

"I'm sorry if I sounded too preachy," Rita apologized. "I didn't mean to give you a lesson in Judaism. Is anything wrong?"

Shirley hopped down from the stool, walked directly to Rita, and put her arms around her friend. "Nothing's wrong at all. I was just appreciating the irony of the fact that it took you, my *Jewish* friend, to remind me, a Christian, the true meaning of Christmas."

Nine

That evening while Stan and the kids were around the dinner table feasting on baked ham and au gratin potatoes, Shirley attempted to lecture them on two thousand years of Jewish history.

No one seemed the least bit interested.

"We saw that Disney movie *The Prince of Egypt*," Stan finally said. "We know all about Moses and the Children of Israel."

Shirley sighed. That had been her attitude six hours ago. "It wasn't a Disney movie," she corrected him gently. "It was produced by Stephen Spielberg—a *Jew*."

"Where did you learn all this stuff anyway?" Stan wanted to know.

"From Rita. Surely, you knew that she is Jewish."

"*Shirley*, I didn't. You never mentioned it before."

"Well she is, and today she taught me a lot about Judaism as well as Christianity."

"That's nice," Stan said between bites of food. "Maybe you can invite her to our company party. Sounds like she could bring some diversity. We could use some diversity."

Shirley brightened. "That might be a good idea. Did you find out when your office party is?"

"December twenty-third."

"Where?"

Stan held his hand to his mouth and coughed. "Here." He nearly choked on the word.

Shirley dropped the forkful of potatoes that was halfway to her mouth. The clatter caught the attention of the children. They all froze still as statues. "Did you say your office Christmas party is going to be *here*? Here at *our* house?"

Stan nodded, but did look up to meet his wife's piercing glare.

"Stanley, how could you do that to me? No one even asked me if it was all right with me. Maybe I have other plans. Did you ever think of that when you volunteered our home?"

"I'm sorry, sweetheart. I tried to call you this afternoon when I got the memo."

"What memo?"

"The one from Curtis that said he understood the importance of a holiday party, but that the budget would not allow for a catered affair. This year he suggested the employees begin taking turns holding the office parties at their homes. That way the budget stays cut and everyone gets better acquainted on a more personal basis."

"That cheapskate. But why *our* house?"

"Curtis put it in the memo without even talking to me. After everyone had gotten their E-mail, he stuck his head in my office and said, 'I hope your wife won't mind us using your house. I'd volunteer mine, but I just had my hardwood floors refinished and don't want to get them scuffed.' "

"What a butthead!" Samantha said.

Neither of her parents disciplined her language, or disagreed with her assessment.

"Sometimes I wish you worked for a huge corporation instead of such a small company," Shirley groaned. "A corporation that would pay for catered affairs. Lobster at the Waterfront Bistro sounds better than Hamburger-Stretcher Casserole in our living room."

Stan forced a smile. "Whatever you prepare, Shirley, will taste delicious."

"No need to kiss up to me now," she said. "Besides, I don't intend to prepare anything. Other people can bring potluck—peanut butter and jelly casseroles, for all I care."

He pushed his plate back and looked down. "I'm sorry. Sorry because there's no pleasing you, no pleasing Curtis."

"Whoa . . ."

He leaned his elbows forward on the table. He didn't sound angry—just resigned. "Shirley, I wish I had a great job, too. I really wish I worked for myself. But you're right. Until Curtis came along last year, I enjoyed being a big fish in a little pond. Now I don't know what to think, to do."

"Are you getting a new job, Daddy?" Samantha wanted to know.

"Of course he isn't." Shirley answered before Stan could. It was one thing to talk about the possibility once in a while, but for Stan to actually quit and lose all his years of seniority was quite another. She didn't know what kind of mood he was in, but she knew she didn't like it.

"Daddy, are you getting fired?" Sean asked when the room remained silent.

"Of course he's not," Shirley quickly settled the matter. Then she winked at Stan and whispered, "You've got to put up with both Curtis and me for a little while longer—at least until after Christmas."

As the season fell into full swing, Shirley felt the pressure. A few check marks dotted her holiday lists, but for the most part, Shirley was aware that she wasn't making much progress toward her goal of a no-stress Christmas season.

She was standing in line one afternoon at the grocery store when she heard the unmistakable and grating voice behind her. It was the voice of Mertyl Casper, a woman who belonged to Shirley's church group. In Shirley's mind, Mertyl was Betty Crocker, Donna Reed, and Peg Bundy all rolled into one. The Peg Bundy part was difficult to explain. The woman was the epitome of middle-America's God-fearing, patriotic, 1950's kind of housewife, but there was something about her. . . . Maybe it was Mertyl's bouffant copper-colored hair or the leopard-print Lycra pants she wore with a cardigan and pearls. Mertyl was also the mother of three, different ages and sizes but identical, matching daughters.

"Hello, Mertyl. How are you?" Shirley surprised herself with the cheerfulness that sprang from her voice.

Mertyl looked at Shirley, then did a quick assessment of the frozen meals and junk foods that were piled high in Shirley's shopping cart. Shirley noted that her fellow parishioner was buying a healthy supply of fresh fruits and vegetables. Celery and Swiss chard appeared to be growing over the sides of her cart.

"Shirley, dear! Are you all ready for Christmas? There are only seventeen shopping days left, you know."

"I know, but I've just gotten started."

Mertyl's mouth fell open, like someone had had just told her Sonny and Cher were no longer a duo.

"Shirley, you've got to be kidding. Waiting until now to get started! Why, I do all my Christmas shopping right on December twenty-sixth each year. That way, I get the best bargains, not to mention a whole year's head start."

"How nice." Shirley winced, cursing the slow-moving line. No matter where Shirley shopped, the clerk for the checkout line she stood in seemed to always be training, doing a price check, or running out of register tape.

"Of course," Mertyl droned, "with all of my growing daughters, I have plenty of sewing to keep me busy all year round. You know how I like to dress all of us in matching outfits."

Shirley nodded, conjuring up the image of a row of twirled lollipops—real suckers.

"Oh, hon, you can't imagine how hard it is to find pink gingham this time of year," Mertyl complained in a high nasal twang.

"No, I really can't."

"Oh, that's right. You don't sew, you poor thing. You'd think I'd remember that after all these years. Do you do much handwork?"

Shirley made a fist, and thought of some *hand*work she would like to do at that exact moment. Instead, she tore open a box of animal crackers and handed one to baby Stephen, who was propped up in the front of the shopping cart. Shirley shook her head at Mertyl and pushed her cart forward, grateful to have finally reached the register. It took another five or six minutes of listening to Mertyl murmur about patterns, crochet hooks, and the inflated price of lace, before Shirley was able to write out her check—with trembling hands.

Mertyl was one of those people who really managed to burrow under Shirley's skin. *Way* under. At least a couple of layers deep. She drove Shirley crazy, and made her feel guilty. *No,* thought Shirley, *Mertyl can't make me feeling anything—I'm the one responsible for how I feel.* The psychologist in her head was once again tapping to get out.

"Merry Christmas," Shirley managed to say, pushing her cart toward the nearest exit.

"Merry Christmas to you, Shirley! We're looking forward to a week from tonight—seven p.m. sharp. Don't be late." She crooked a bony warning finger in Shirley's direction.

Shirley pulled the cart to a jerky halt. "What's a week from tonight?"

Mertyl laughed. It sounded like a BB gun popping. "Oh, honey, you are a kidder, all right. I heard from Pastor Dalebout's wife that you're going to do a great job as chairwoman of the church Christmas social."

Shirley cursed.

"Pardon me!" Mertyl clapped her hands against both cheeks. "What did you say?"

"I said a woman can't get any luckier!" she lied.

Shirley hadn't forgotten. Really, she hadn't. She'd already done most of the preparatory work; she just hadn't realized that she only had one week left to wrap up all the loose ends. It was always easier to be a grunt laborer than to push the grunts. Somehow Shirley always ended up grunting *and* pushing.

"I hear it's going to be an old-fashioned affair with a real cakewalk and a talent contest," Mertyl bellowed across the store. "My girls will be singing. You won't be able to miss them, in their matching dresses. I just hope I can find enough pink gingham in time."

"I'm sure you will," Shirley croaked, yanking her shopping cart out of the automatic door that nearly had it pinned. Before Shirley managed her way completely out of the store, Mertyl yelled one last piece of unsettling information.

"I hear you're entering Stephen in the annual cute-baby contest. You'd better stay on my good side because I'm head of the judging committee this year, Shirley, hon."

Where's a Jew when you need a good Christian attitude? Shirley thought, wondering why it was so difficult to merely be nice to some people.

After the grocery store, she swung by Sara's preschool.

"Please thank your husband for us," Sara's teacher, Mrs. Wilcox, said as they were leaving. "That was so kind of him to volunteer."

Shirley stopped in her tracks. "Excuse me?"

Mrs. Wilcox smiled coyly. "Don't be so modest, dear. Your family has always gone the extra mile to help support your children. But when Sara said her father had agreed to play Santa

Claus at our holiday party, well, that was way above the call of duty."

Shirley gazed down at Sara, who was grinning with innocence and enthusiasm.

"When is the school's party?" Shirley asked hesitantly.

"One week from tonight. Seven p.m. Sara should be here fifteen minutes early, since she is singing in the choir, but of course you already knew that—all the information was on that green note I passed out last week."

Shirley couldn't remember any green note, and didn't have a clue what Mrs. Wilcox was talking about, but Shirley wasn't about to let the whole world know what a negligent mother she was.

Once they were alone in the car, Shirley turned to Sara. "Honey, when did Daddy volunteer to play Santa for your school?"

"He hasn't yet."

Shirley sighed. "That's what I thought."

"But he will," Sara chimed confidently. "Daddy said Santa needs all of the helpers he can get."

"Santa's not the only one who needs help.

Little did Shirley realize just how *much* help she was really going to need until later that night, when Samantha informed her that *The Nutcracker*'s opening night had been changed—"To one week from tonight. At seven p.m., sharp."

"Hey, that's when my piano recital is," Sean bellowed. "I told you that a month ago."

"What's the matter, Shirley?" Stan asked, pulling out a kitchen chair for Shirley to sit down on. "You look like you don't feel well."

Shirley groaned. "So much for my stress-free holiday season! So much for my calendar planning! Do you realize that Sean's piano recital is the same night and time as Samantha's premier *Nutcracker* performance *and* our church social? But then you get to miss them all because you'll be jingling bells for Sara's preschool Christmas party."

Stan stared at her. "*What* are you talking about?"

Shirley recited what Mrs. Wilcox had said.

He didn't seem too surprised—in fact, he seemed amused.

Stan grinned at her, then said rather seriously, "Did I mention that Curtis moved our office party to a week from tonight—seven p.m., sharp?"

Shirley suddenly turned the color of chalk. "I think I'm going to be sick."

Stan quickly skidded his own chair away. "Just kidding, sweetheart. Just kidding."

Ten

Shirley had never felt so torn or stressed in her life, at least not that she could recall. How could such a scheduling conflict have actually occurred? *How* didn't really matter at this point.

"Next year I'll have everyone clear their plans with me first," she promised herself aloud, as she was getting ready to face the week from hell. For the first, and *only* time, she actually felt jealous of Mertyl Casper, who had had her presents purchased and wrapped for months. Mertyl never would have stood for such chaos.

Once the kids were at school and Stephen was down for his morning nap, Shirley knew she had no time to waste. She sat at her computer and reworked her three holiday lists into one. Some sacrifices had to be made. All the time and energy she was going to volunteer to the community now looked like it was going to be consumed by her own family. Oh, well. Then she tried to think of ways she could finagle herself to be at Sara's preschool, Samantha's *Nutcracker*, Sean's recital, and the church social—all within the same sixty-minute time window. Even if she had Jane Jetson's space car, there was no way she would be able to spread herself so thin and so fast.

Which child would have to do without her? Which child would miss her the least? She felt grateful that Stan was the kind of father who was more than willing to fill in. Shirley wished that she could engrave those precious moments of Stan's goodness forever in her memory, and then recall them at those heated times when she was wondering why she had ever said, "I do." She supposed that was what "being there for each other" really meant—sometimes being there when the other one could not.

Shirley also had a lot of extra work to do for her own desktop publishing business. Sometimes she wished it wasn't doing quite as well as it was. The reason she worked at home was so that she could be with the kids, but she was coming to understand that being there in body did not always mean being there.

Right next to Shirley's desk was a frame that she periodically filled with thoughts to motivate her. Her current inspirational quote had been framed for more than a month. It was attributed to Jacqueline Kennedy Onassis:

> If you bungle raising your children, I don't think whatever else you do will matter very much.

Shirley didn't want to bungle the raising of her children. Nor did she want to be less than a passionate and devoted wife. A brilliant business woman. A devout Christian. A better daughter. An improved poker player and a time-traveler. And more than ever, Shirley longed to be young and skinny. Rita-skinny.

For now, she felt forced to settle for being a mere mortal, incapable of perfection. That realization didn't stop her desires, nor squelch her pangs of guilt. Too much to do and not enough time or energy to go around. It was the only time in years that there wasn't enough Shirley to go around.

Shirley had called Stan's office and had gotten the information about his company party. Thankfully, she would not have to worry about that until this crazy week had ended.

There were still presents to buy. Packages to wrap. Letters to write and, of course, the family Christmas picture to take. Shirley wondered what would happen if Christmas came and went, and she never got all of her items checked off. Would the world end? She was submerged in thought when the telephone rang.

"Hello, Shirley. This is Mrs. Gleed from down the street. I hope I'm not bothering you."

"Not at all," responded Shirley, feeling her day rapidly brighten. Mrs. Gleed was Shirley's inspiration. The woman was pushing ninety, but ran circles around women Shirley's age, or at least around Shirley. Nellie Gleed was everything Shirley wanted to be. She did the things that Shirley only dreamed of, like challenging Wyoming's white-water rapids and taking piano lessons, though society told her she was decades past her prime.

"I was just here in my kitchen dipping homemade chocolates, and I thought of you and your precious little family. Do you remember last year when you said you would like to learn to make homemade candy?"

"I sure do. No fancy boxed chocolates can compare to yours, Nellie."

"Well, thank you, dear. I've been doing this for more years than you've been alive. If you would like to pop by, I'll be happy to share a few secret family recipes with you."

Shirley felt her shoulders sag. Another opportunity she would love to take advantage of, but there was no way.

"I'm sorry. I wish I could come by. It's just that my baby is asleep, and I've got a pile of work to do, and a million Christmas errands to finish. 'Tis the season to go crazy, you know."

Mrs. Gleed chuckled. "I understand, dear. Is there anything I can do to help you?"

"Not unless you're one of Santa's elves." Shirley laughed and then offered a brief overview of the demands she was facing.

"I understand," Mrs. Gleed repeated, slowly and empathetically. "I'll save you a homemade turtle. I know how you love caramel and pecans."

"Thank you, my friend. Merry Christmas."

Shirley had been back working at her computer for less than an hour when the doorbell rang. It was Nellie Gleed, an approaching-ancient angel, loaded down with a huge platter of hand-dipped chocolates.

"Come in," Shirley ushered, maybe a little too enthusiastically, but truly grateful for the company, not to mention the candy.

"You sounded so overburdened," said Mrs. Gleed, "I thought I'd bring you a little Christmas cheer." With that, she handed Shirley the candy, then took off her coat to reveal that she was wearing an apron. "I've come to help you, dear. I'll start with the dishes and then make my way through the rest of the house."

"Oh, no," Shirley protested, touched by the gesture, but embarrassed because her house really did need the touch of an angel. "I know my house is a mess. I used to have a girl that came in every once in a while. I think I wore her out. Since then, I haven't been able to stay on top of my job and the housework, not to mention my family."

Mrs. Gleed walked to the hall closet and hung up her coat. "Where's your broom?" she asked.

Shirley wasn't about to let this woman, older than her own grandmother, clean her house. Not Nellie Gleed. But telling the woman no and getting her to stop were two very different tasks.

"Quit feeling like you owe the world a ride on your shoulders, Shirley. You deserve a little pick-me-up once in a while."

"I know, but it's just that—"

"You can do me one favor," interrupted Mrs. Gleed. "You can go to my car and bring me my basket of cleaning supplies. I like to use my own rags. I cut up my dead husband's underwear. It's not like he's going to be needing them or anything. My, but those rags can make a mirror shine!"

Shirley grinned and fetched the basket of cleaning supplies. Then Shirley and Nellie worked together for the next hour, polishing and shining, vacuuming and picking up. They didn't stop until Stephen woke up from his nap.

Nellie insisted on rocking him. She played with Stephen while Shirley finished a report she was preparing for one of her clients.

"I haven't had this productive a day in years," Shirley admitted appreciatively as the two women shared a can of soup and a package of soda crackers for lunch.

"I'm glad that I could help, dear."

Shirley leaned toward Mrs. Gleed and placed a hand on the woman's arm."Where do you get your endless supply of energy?"

"Well, I have to admit, I am feeling a bit spryer these days. It's my ab device, Shirley dear."

Shirley put a hunk of cheddar cheese on a cracker and popped it into her mouth. "Your what?" she asked, spewing a few crumbs.

"It's one of those machines you've seen advertised on television. I bought one a few months ago, and I do my fifteen minutes every morning and another ten or fifteen minutes at night. I get right down on the floor and do my situps and leg lifts."

Without warning, Mrs. Gleed dropped to the floor and began demonstrating. "Of course, I don't look like the young girl on the video, but I don't look too shabby in my leopard leotard."

Shirley wanted to laugh, but Mrs. Gleed was serious.

"Yes, dear. My friends all wonder if I am eating right because I've lost a few pounds. Actually, I allow them to worry about me a little. Why, that nice widower across from my house has actually been making eyes at me. I swear it."

Shirley didn't doubt it to be true. Mrs. Gleed had the look of a much, much younger woman and the spirit of a teenager.

Nellie insisted on staying until the lunch dishes were washed and put away. When she departed, the house was clean, the baby was happy, and Shirley was shrouded in appreciative awe.

Shirley had talked a lot about service during the past months, and she always gave a lot of if-you-ever-need-me-just-call kind of help. But people like Rita and Mrs. Gleed were teaching Shirley that service was never convenient, but when you came to *really* help a friend, you wore an apron.

For the rest of the day, and even into the night, Shirley felt happy. It showed.

"How come you're so different?" Sean asked his mother.

Shirley ran her hand across her son's gelled buzz cut. It was sticking out like ornery blades of unruly grass. "Because I found out today that Santa Claus hasn't forgotten your dear old mother. He sent one of his best elves today to help me."

Samantha shook her head and whispered, "Mom, I hate to break it to you, but there is no Santa Claus."

Sara came into the room at just that moment. "There is too a Santa, isn't there, Mommy?"

Shirley looked into the eyes of her three oldest children, one child at a time. "Yes, Virginia, there is a Santa Claus," she testified.

"Who's Virginia?" they all wanted to know.

She shook her head. "Come on, kids. It's story time."

"But what about the dinner dishes?" asked Samantha, whose turn it was to do them.

"They'll wait," said Shirley. "The dishes will always wait."

Eleven

Ever since Samantha was a baby, one of Shirley's most cherished holiday traditions was story time. She had always loved reading to her children, or *with* them, now that Sami and Sean could read. At Christmas though, story time to Shirley, approached the sacred. Too often, during the everydayness of the year, story time was pushed aside. Not at Christmas.

At first the only books they had to share were ones they borrowed from the local library and a personal dog-eared copy of Charles Dickens' *A Christmas Carol*. Since then, at least one book every year had been added to her personal library. Even when Samantha had been just a few months old, Shirley had read to her. Now that she was a teenager, those hours and purchases were paying off.

Samantha, Sean, Sara, and even little Stephen all piled onto the bed with Shirley. They pulled the comforter around them and fought over the pillows. When everyone was finally settled, Shirley took a book from a tall stack of Christmas stories piled on the nightstand next to her bed.

"I wonder which new book to ask Santa for this year," Shirley mused aloud.

Sean wedged himself closer to his mother. "Do you get a Christmas book *every* year?"

"I have since Samantha was born."

"Which one is your favorite story?" Sara asked.

"I don't know. Which one do *you* like?" Shirley inquired, but already knew that her daughter would choose Dr. Seuss' masterpiece.

"*How the Grinch Stole Christmas*!" Sara shouted at the top of her lungs.

"Shhhh, or you'll scare Stephen," Samantha warned, but the

outburst didn't seem to disturb the baby. He lay on the pillow next to his mother, content and quiet. His response, or lack of it, didn't go unnoticed by Shirley, but she told herself he was just sleepy.

"My favorite story is the *real* Christmas story from St. Luke," said Samantha. "Can I be the one to read it tonight?"

Shirley smiled at her eldest daughter, who was growing up by the day. Shirley didn't want to miss a minute of it. "Of course you can, sweetheart."

"I want you to read *Why Christmas Trees Aren't Perfect.*" Sean, too, requested his favorite.

"We read that one last night," said Sara.

"So. We can read it again tonight," Sean insisted.

"What if we begin with *The Gift of the Magi*?" suggested Shirley, since it was one of her personal favorites.

"Okay," the kids agreed, snuggling close to their mother.

Seven stories later, no one wanted to quit. So homework and housework were set aside while Shirley and her children made their way to the North Pole and back. It was past ten when the story of the very first Christmas transported them two thousand years back in time to a little town called Bethlehem. . . .

The next few days found Shirley abuzz with a million and one errands. Her mind and body felt exhausted, but she kept the potpourri simmering so the house continually smelled like cinnamon. The decorations remained hung, at least the ones Sara couldn't reach. Every time she tried to blame the damage on her little brother, Shirley could not help wishing that Stephen *was* the one responsible for an aggressive interest in all of the brightly-colored, shimmering ornaments. His disinterest was like a shadow that dogged her, darkening her spirits, but she only moved faster, trying to keep ahead of her fears.

One of the highlights of her day came with the mail. She quickly sorted through the bills to find the Christmas-colored envelopes. Shirley loved the annual greetings from family and friends. Her favorite cards included photos and Christmas letters. She was reading a letter from her almost-forgotten cousin when her mother knocked on the door.

There stood Lena draped in crushed velvet the color of

pomegranates. "I'm feeling Christmassy. Let's go to the mall," she suggested.

Shirley's hands involuntarily touched her hair. She had barely run a brush through it. "I don't have time, Mom."

"Sure you do. I know that Sara doesn't have to be picked up from preschool for a few hours, and Stephen can come with us."

"But I have a deadline to meet."

"You'll meet it. You always do. Now grab your coat and come on."

Shirley looked at her mother. This was so unlike the woman. "What's with the spontaneity, Mom? You usually plan every shopping trip weeks in advance."

"My therapist said a little spur-of-the-moment living is good for me."

"Your *therapist*? I had no idea you were back in therapy." About a year ago, Shirley had gone through a simple validation exercise with her mother. It had helped their relationship, but more than that, it had been the start of a new woman, a mother Shirley sometimes did not know.

"I think I like this new you, Mom."

"So do I. Now come on, let's go. I'll get Stephen dressed."

"He *is* dressed."

"He can't wear that outfit to the mall. It's stained."

"He'll have a coat over it, Mother. No one will see."

Lena lifted Stephen and took him down the hall to change him into something *more appropriate*.

When they emerged, Stephen was wearing his Sunday outfit, a gray tweed vest and white shirt. His hair was damp and slicked back. "Don't you have any black shoes for him?"

"What's wrong with the brown shoes he was wearing?"

"Shirley, you inherited your father's fashion sense—or lack of it."

Shirley was tempted to argue, but knew better. It was the first time Lena had mentioned her father in months, maybe even a year. He was still a subject mother and daughter could not discuss without pain and conflict.

Shirley exhaled with resignation. "We can buy Stephen a pair at the Five-Buck Shoe Store at the mall."

"He'll need new socks, too," Lena turned the dagger. "All the ones you have for him are dirty."

"They are not dirty. The are dingy, and dingy is not the same as dirty, Mother."

Lena raised her eyebrows. "Shirley, you buy the shoes and I'll spring for a pair of white socks, what do you say to that?"

Shirley smiled. "Mom, maybe you haven't changed that much after all."

Shirley was not exactly comfortable with the idea of taking off and going to the mall with her mother, but for a pair of free socks—why not?

The afternoon turned out to be rather pleasant. As soon as they had purchased new shoes and clean white socks for Stephen, the tension eased, and Shirley got some holiday shopping done for her children. Then she bought her mother a sweater. Navy blue with purple flowers. Cream lace on the collar. It wasn't anything Shirley would have selected.

"I love it!" said her mother.

"I'm glad, Mom. You're the one who chose it. Merry Christmas."

"Oh, don't give it to me just yet. Wrap it and give it to me with the presents the kids make me. That way Christmas still feels special to me."

"Okay, Mom. I will. Just promise to act surprised."

"Don't I always?"

They passed two or three huge mounds of Monster Mountain Mashers.

"What are those toys that look like half truck and half monster?" Shirley's mother asked.

"They are what Sean wants for Christmas. They transform from animal to machine and back again."

"In my childhood, after Roosevelt was president, the Teddy Bear was the rage. But let me advise you dear, if you haven't already bought a monster crusher toy for little Sean, you had better do it now before they are all gone."

"I haven't bought his yet," Shirley admitted. "He's desperate for a blue one. But if I buy it now, he'll find it and won't be surprised. That kid is the worst snoop. I caught him unwrapping presents in my closet last year, trying to rewrap before he was found out."

"Maybe you should find a better hiding place."

"I've tried. He's got a sixth sense that leads him to find any hidden present—Christmas, birthday, you name it, he can find it."

"Well, you better buy his masher toy today, or you might not get one."

Shirley laughed. "Mom, nobody else wants them except Sean. For weeks I've been seeing stacks of them in every store. Even the grocery store sells them. Trust me, they won't be like Cabbage Patch Dolls. The supply will outlast the demand."

Shirley's mother just smiled, the same *I-know-better-than-you-know* smile that Shirley had used on her own children.

Just as they were leaving, they ran into Rita, who was at the mall shopping for the children at the shelter. Even though Rita never made an issue of it, Shirley knew these shopping sprees were common for Rita. *Giving* was her second nature.

"We've got to get together soon," Rita said, sounding sincere. "Something nondenominational," she joked.

"If I make it past this week, we'll get together to celebrate the season," Shirley promised.

"Hectic week, huh?" Rita asked innocently.

Shirley suddenly felt her bottom lip begin to quiver. Right there, in the middle of the mall, she felt like she was about to explode, like a firecracker inside of a jack-o'-lantern. Rita cupped Shirley's elbow while Lena guided the stroller to a nearby vacant bench.

They all sat down and Shirley poured out her soul, releasing pressure like steam from a tea kettle. She tried to explain her dilemma—how so many important events were scheduled for the same evening. She told them about her lists and all of the efforts she had made to make this holiday her best one yet. How she had failed miserably.

Lena patted Shirley's shoulder. "It sounds like you've taken on far too much, Shirley. You know you always do that. You have got to learn to prioritize."

"You're right, Mom. But how do I reorganize my top priorities when they are *all* equally important?"

"I'll take Sean to his recital," Rita volunteered. "I'd love to hear him play the piano."

Shirley wiped a tear from her cheek. "He still plays *Jolly Old St. Nicholas* with one finger," Shirley found herself reluctantly apologizing, then passing judgment. "I don't think it will be the kind of concert you're used to attending."

Rita looked hurt for one flashing moment, but then smiled. "I think it sounds refreshing."

"Really?"

Lena jabbed Shirley sharply in the ribs. "The woman is trying to help. Rita is your friend. I've known that since I first met her months ago. You're lucky Rita is in your life. You need help and she wants to help. What is wrong with you, girl?"

"Okay," Shirley yielded, feeling both relief and gratitude. "Sean will be thrilled to have you there, Rita. You know how all of my kids adore you, and now I guess my mother does, too."

"I'll be at the opening night of *The Nutcracker* to see Sami dance," Lena reminded Shirley. "I'll save your seats until you can get through at the church social and Stan can finish at Sara's preschool. I know Sami will understand. She's not a child anymore."

Shirley looked first into her mother's eyes and then into her friend's. Here she was, flanked on either side by women who cared about her and her family. When would she learn the lesson that life had been trying to pound into her for so many years—she didn't have to shoulder the weight of the world alone. All she had to do was ask for help. That, for Shirley, had always been next to impossible.

"Thanks, you two," she softly sobbed. "I've been feeling so sorry for myself. I was torn. I didn't know what I was going to do." She sat up and grinned. "Now I do—I'm going to buy us all a late lunch!"

At Rita's suggestion, they went to a kosher deli near the mall.

"What should I order?" Lena asked, sounding uncertain of her surroundings.

"Order anything you'd like," Rita put her at ease, then grinned at Shirley. "Just not a ham sandwich."

Lena laughed. "Even *I* know that Jews don't eat pork."

Shirley stepped closer to her mother. "Who told *you* that Rita is Jewish?"

"Nobody told me. Nobody needed to tell me. What kind of an idiot couldn't figure that one out?"

Shirley stepped back and hung her head. "I can't imagine," she lied.

Twelve

Shirley headed home warmed by the spirit and sentiments of both Christmas and Thanksgiving. There were people in her life whom she could count on—people for whom she was so grateful, and yet didn't always know it, let alone show it. The mental list she was writing was short. As far as friends for whom to be grateful, Rita's name topped the list. Someday, Shirley vowed, the tables would turn, and Shirley would be the one helping Rita, instead of it always being the other way around.

More and more, Shirley was also beginning to appreciate her own mother, in spite of their diversity, or maybe *because* of it. Shirley would never admit it to Lena, but she realized that her mother still had a great deal to teach her.

Shirley's mother-in-law, no doubt, also had a lot to offer, but Shirley had to admit that she was not the most pliable student under that woman's tutelage. She never felt she was good enough when she was around her mother-in-law. It might have had something to do with the fact she'd told Shirley as much. There wasn't a big difference between the inadequacy Shirley felt around Lena versus her mother-in-law, but yet, there was. Lena was her mother; they were bound by blood. A simple divorce decree, her mother-in-law had once informed her, would sever all their family ties.

"Oh, you're making too much of Mom's moods," Stan tried to convince Shirley. "You never feel like you measure up to anyone. Learn to ignore what other people think of you; worry about what you think of yourself."

Easy advice to give, not so easy to take.

It was still three days before *The Nutcracker* opened. Shirley was making progress, but in order to keep on top of all she had to do, she did her computer work and housecleaning at night, while Stan and the kids caught up on their sleep. During the day she burned tankfuls of gasoline and inches of rubber off her car's tread, driving her children to various destinations around town.

They each had their own shopping lists and budgets to blow, too. Normally, Stan would have helped more, but Curtis kept him swamped with added work. After the new year, something would have to be done about that situation. She knew Stan was just holding out until the holidays were over for the sake of the family.

The lost sleep was beginning to take its toll. The bags under Shirley's eyes were the size of Easter eggs, only not as colorful. In spite of telling herself everything would work out, Shirley felt the pressure once again, building to the point of explosion. She would have called someone for assistance, but there were just too many tasks that required her personal attention.

Her temper grew shorter by the minute, and she often found herself typing the same sentences over and over. One night just as she finished a document for a favored client, Shirley accidentally pushed the Delete key when she meant to press the Save key. There was a safety device built into her computer program, but even that, she had mistakenly overridden.

"Aren't computers dumb?" Stan said. "They should know you didn't mean *delete*, even though you said so . . . twice!"

"If you're trying to make me feel better, it's not working."

"Why are you so ornery? Shirley, you can find some way to reduce your schedule."

"And what do you suggest that I give up, Stanley?" Her voice quivered with raw emotion. "Sami's *Nutcracker* . . . Sean's piano lessons . . . Sara's school program . . . my work? Maybe I could forgo cooking and cleaning around here, or getting everything ready for Christmas."

"What about the church social?" he proposed. "Why do *you* have to be in it?"

"Because I volunteered and they are counting on me," she answered more abruptly than she intended. "Besides, Stephen is starring in the baby contest. And for your information, I already called Pastor Dalebout and he said they couldn't find anyone else to do the cakewalk or help pass out the treat bags for the children."

"Weren't you supposed to do the invitations as well?"

"Already done. I dropped them off at the church last Sunday."

Stan embraced his wife, the bear-hug tight way that made her feel like everything was going to somehow be okay.

"You amaze me, Shirley. I don't know where you find the time and energy to accomplish all that you do. You realize I support you, don't you?"

"I guess so," she replied, wondering exactly what he meant by "support."

"If you need anything, all you have to do is let me know. I'll be there."

"Wearing an apron?" she asked, picturing Nellie Gleed standing on their doorstep, clad in service attire.

"What?"

"Forget it. You wouldn't understand."

Later Shirley was wrapping a pair of socks for Stan when his mother called on the telephone. She needed to go do some Christmas shopping and wondered if Shirley was going downtown any time soon.

Shirley knew that her mother-in-law was capable of driving herself, but congested traffic made her nervous, and Shirley really didn't mind helping her out. Just not this week.

"I'm swamped with *The Nutcracker* and all," Shirley explained gently, but firmly. "Remember I told you how many events we've got going on the same night. I'm trying to get ready for them all, but next week I should have some free time; I'll be happy to drive you downtown then."

Her mother-in-law huffed into the receiver. "Don't worry about it, Shirley. By then it will be too late. The sale will be over."

"What sale?"

"The one that ends today."

Shirley caved, and spent the rest of the day driving her mother-in-law from store to store, weaving through the insanity of downtown Christmas traffic.

"I don't think the inching along, bumper to bumper, will kill me," she muttered to herself, "but trying to find a parking place downtown during the holiday season probably will. If I don't crash the car, I'll die of a heart attack brought on by stress."

"What are you saying?" Shirley's mother-in-law asked.

"Oh, nothing, Mom."

"Shirley, you realize you talk to yourself. I don't think that's a good sign."

"Sign of what?" Shirley asked with the phoniest smile she could plaster across her mug. She pulled the car over to the curb to let her mother-in-law out at the store that was hosting the all-important sale. "I'll keep circling the block, and meet you right back here as soon as you're ready."

After Shirley's fourth time around the block, her mother-in-law returned to the car, sans packages.

"Can't you find anything you like?"

"Not a thing. The sale was a farce. It's all trash. Nothing worth buying. I hate the colors this season. They are so bright and unnatural-looking."

Shirley knew better than to disagree. "Can I drive you somewhere else, Mom?" She regretted the invitation the minute it passed her lips.

"Yes. I'd like to go to the mall."

"The mall? You mean the one by our house? The one we passed on our way here?"

"If it's not too much trouble for you. I wouldn't want to put you out or anything."

Shirley gritted her teeth, determined to make the best of a bad situation. She had been preaching to herself about true service ever since Nellie Gleed had demonstrated it. Now Shirley had to practice what she'd been preaching.

"No trouble at all," she fibbed, trying not to grimace. "I just have to pick the kids up, run a few errands, then we can all go with you to the mall. The kids have been wanting to go anyway, and I still have some shopping left to do."

The woman struggled with her seat belt, then turned to Shirley. "I certainly hope you're going to buy yourself some new clothes, Shirley. It's not like you don't need them."

Shirley's mind flashed red, the words "frumpy" and "strangle" taking turns blinking. She looked down at her worn sneakers, ragged stretch pants, and maternity sweater. As much as it hurt, her mother-in-law was right. If clothes made the woman, what did that make Shirley?

While the kids were off shopping the mall stores with Grandma, Shirley went to the women's apparel section of a department store and purchased two new outfits. She immediately felt guilty for spending so much money on herself, but then remembered, it wasn't money—it was *credit*! As long as the charge card wasn't declined, Shirley was determined to have a very merry Christmas. She was almost out of the store when her eye noticed the display. It was a silk Christmas tree decorated with bright lights and a thousand hanging brassieres. This batch was called *Fantasy Bras*.

"May I help you?" A clerk appeared automatically by Shirley's side. It was a young man with a pierced nose and bright green eyeliner.

"Are these bras really as wonderful as the advertising?"

"Absolutely!" he said with conviction. "They can do wonders for all shapes, or even full-figured gals like yourself."

She chose to take the "full-figured" comment as a compliment. Besides, she *was* full-figured. That was the one positive physical side effect of having a baby. Shirley's chest swelled a few cup sizes. She might as well enjoy it while it lasted, which was always about exactly the same amount of time that she nursed her babies. Stephen was taking a bottle more frequently, so Shirley grabbed the biggest bra from the tree.

"Tell me about this one," she instructed the clerk, who was now curling his tongue to reveal that it, too, was pierced. She tried not to speculate on what other parts of his body boasted an extra hole or two.

"You're holding our very newest bra," gushed the man. "It's specially made to add support and lift to breasts that are losing their fight with gravity." He laughed at his own joke until he realized that he was laughing alone.

"This feels like it's got enough wire to circle the planet." Shirley was scrutinizing the bra in detail. "Is it comfortable?"

"They do have a lot of wire, but they need it. You're welcome to try one on," he invited. "We have some *testers* in the dressing room."

The thought of putting her bare breasts into public-access cups made her shudder. "No, no, thank you. I think I'll just buy this one. It looks like it will fit just fine."

The guy ogled her, grinning. Shirley didn't know whether to be flattered or not.

"May your cups runneth over," were the last words he said as he snatched the credit card from her hand.

* * *

As Shirley pulled into her mother-in-law's driveway, the woman announced, "I bought your family's Christmas present when we were at the mall."

"Really? I didn't think you bought a thing," said Shirley. "You aren't carrying any packages."

"Well, I did," she snorted, shifting her weight from one side to the other. "What I really needed was a new tube of Preparation H, but there wasn't a drugstore around."

"I'll pick you some up next time I go to Wal-Mart," Shirley said quickly, heading her off before she requested a ride to the drugstore.

Her mother-in-law waved an envelope toward Shirley. "I'd like to wait until Christmas to give it to you," she said, "but I want you to use it before then."

Shirley's curiosity was peaked. "What is it?"

"It's a gift certificate. You have to use it right away."

Touché! That's what Shirley had bought her last Mother's Day, then again for her birthday, and now for this Christmas as well.

"I've never heard of a gift certificate that expires so soon."

"I never said it expired. I said you have to use it right away. It's a certificate to have your family's picture taken in the mall. If you use it right away, you can order a copy of your family picture for our Christmas present."

Shirley half hugged her mother-in-law as she accepted a piece of paper. "I've been wanting to get our family picture taken. Thanks so much."

The friendly moment was a bit unnatural for both of them. Shirley hurriedly backed away. The kids in the backseat were grumbling about having to have a "stupid picture taken."

Her mother-in-law grunted her way out of the car. "The people at the photo studio recommended that you coordinate your clothing."

Shirley smiled, glad for her new outfits, especially her new bra. "I know just what I'll wear," she announced confidently.

"Shirley, I have a personal suggestion. Wear black. It makes you look thinner."

Thirteen

Soon after she got home, Shirley looked into the mirror. She had been too harried to notice before, but how could she have missed it? There stood before her an old, tired, fat, and strangely unfamiliar woman. She was bigger than her husband, and looked older than her mother. Shirley leaned against the bathroom wall, letting her body slide down until she was crumpled, a heap of weary, worn humanity, slouched in the corner. There she stayed, utterly miserable, until the door banged open and Sara marched in.

"The baby's stinky! You need to change him, Mommy."

"I'll be there in a minute, honey."

A loud crash sounded from downstairs.

"Is everything all right?" Shirley called out, concerned.

"No!" Sean yelled. "Sami hit me with the vacuum hose. I think my nose is broken."

"What's going on down there?" Shirley demanded, refusing to rise, even though Sara was tugging at her.

"Get up, Mommy. Let's go see what those troublemakers are up to now."

"Sean's a spoiled brat!" Samantha screeched. "I hate him!"

Sean suddenly cried out in pain.

"Stop it!" Shirley ordered, forcing her bulk upward and thundering down the stairs, two at a time, Sara trying to keep up.

"Yeah, you two. Here comes Mama Rhino," Sara warned her squabbling siblings.

Shirley shot her a quizzical look, but Sara just shrugged. "You know we call you that, Mom."

A few more yelps ascended from the family room.

"You two, stop yelling this instant!" Shirley yelled as loud as she could, noting the irony, but not caring. She then ordered Samantha to vacuum the family room and Sean to put in an extra thirty minutes practicing the piano. They griped, but Shirley glowered, "Don't mess with Mama Rhino."

Shirley changed Stephen's stinky diaper, washed her hands, helped Sara write a letter to the real "North Pole" Santa Claus, changed another diaper, scrubbed her hands again, helped Sean with his piano recital piece, replaced the vacuum bag, answered the phone twice, and washed her hands for the third time before she put dinner on the stove to cook.

When Stan came home, he sat right down in front of the television. "I'm tired," he announced. "It's been one of those days."

"I know," said Shirley, staring down at her cracked and bleeding knuckles.

As the week wore down, she came to realize that Christmas was going to come and go whether she had all of her lists completed or not. It seemed that for every item she checked off, a new one needed to be added.

Rita called her a few times. "I'm worried about you, Shirley. You're not your usual happy self."

"I'm just a little overwhelmed with all I have to do," she admitted. "I'll be all right once we get past this week."

"Remember, you've got people who love you and who will be happy to help if you need us."

"I know. I appreciate what you're doing to help out on Saturday night. Taking Sean to his recital means a lot to all of us. In fact, all of the children fought over who would get to go with *Aunt* Rita."

"I like feeling needed. This is as helpful to me as it is to you."

The confession surprised Shirley. "I thought you were the original woman of independent means."

Rita sighed. "I thought I was, too. But I'm not. I sometimes envy all you have."

Shirley immediately thought of Rita's high-rise condo and maid service. Her bank account had never been overdrawn, and she had a family that didn't demand her every waking moment, not to mention half of her sleeping ones. She thought of how highly people esteemed Rita. She thought of Rita's youthful, skinny, regal appearance.

"Envy *me*, huh? That's a good one. How are your Hanukkah plans coming?"

She imagined she heard Rita mutter, "What plans?" Instead Rita slowly explained, "This is the first year I've observed it for a very long time."

"Really? Why?"

"Because my faith hasn't exactly been unshakable. For a long time, I wondered if there was even a God at all."

This was the most Rita had ever revealed about her inner self. The woman had a story to tell, all right—more like an entire novel. But Rita was only willing to tell it one page at a time, and as much as Shirley wanted her to read faster, she refrained from pushing.

"I think there are times when even stalwart firm believers have to wonder. I've always felt that active faith questions."

Rita paused. "I suppose so, but I know in my heart that God *is* real. I'm fuzzy on the details, but I know that this old world didn't just *big-bang* its way into existence."

Shirley agreed, and for half an hour, the two friends discussed the depths of their souls. They dared to trod taboo territory—religion.

Rita still didn't reveal *why* her faith had been challenged, but she did say that it had been. Something had happened in Rita's past that made her break away, cut ties with most of her family, and keep her physical, as well as emotional, distance from just about everyone. Without warning, their conversation careened.

"Do you know what you need, Shirley?"

"Yeah, I need a credit card that pays itself off every thirty days," she joked.

"No . . . you need a body work-over."

"A what?"

"Whenever I'm feeling really down, I go to the spa and work out, then I get a massage and a facial. A manicure and pedicure are optional."

"Wow. The planet you come from sounds really nice."

"No, really," Rita insisted. "There is nothing like a little pampering to help pick up a woman's spirits."

"Maybe I'll give my hairstylist, Debbie, a call," said Shirley. "We're supposed to have our family picture taken tomorrow and I could use some help with my hair. It's looking a lot like Sean's football helmet."

Rita laughed, and when she finally hung up, Shirley was feeling more optimistic than she had since her last encounter with Rita.

When Shirley called her hair salon, she got the bad news: Debbie had moved. Debbie was the *one* stylist who understood Shirley, and could make her look and feel better about herself with just a cut and color.

"When did she move?" Shirley demanded.

"Six months ago."

"That's impossible. I've been in to have my hair done since then."

"According to our records it's been a little over six months, ma'am."

"Well, Debbie didn't tell me she was moving."

"She got another job and didn't give anyone much notice. She's working at a private salon in Aspen, Colorado."

Shirley could just picture, five-foot-eight, 110-pound Debbie as a ski bunny. The image fit like Lycra.

"Who replaced Debbie?"

"Randall," answered the receptionist.

"A *man*?"

"Yes. He's wonderful. He came to our salon from Newport Beach, California, and he's a master at color."

"Does he have any openings tomorrow?"

"I'm afraid not. He's booked until after the first of the year."

"You're kidding." Shirley didn't try to hide her disappointment. "What am I going to do? We're supposed to have our family picture taken tomorrow and I haven't had anything done to my hair in months, but you already know that."

The receptionist obviously felt sorry for Shirley, or just wanted to get her off the line. "Randall could fit you in at seven-thirty."

"But our appointment is for six-thirty tomorrow night."

"Seven-thirty a.m., ma'am."

"A.m.? As in, in the morning?" Shirley hesitated only a moment before saying, "I'll take it."

Shirley rose the next morning, showered, and did her best to style her own hair. She wasn't about to let Randall, a total stranger, see her with *morning hair*. She managed a couple of coats of mascara and ran the nub of a lipstick tube across her bottom lip, then smashed her lips together in a feeble attempt to blend them evenly. She made a mental note to pick up a new tube of lipstick when she went to the drugstore for her mother-in-law's Preparation H.

She also reminded Stan that he was in charge of getting the older kids to school and Stephen to the baby-sitter, then she got in the car and drove to the salon. She felt guilty for taking this time for herself, but hoped that Rita was right—the investment would pay off.

Randall proved to be everything he had been billed—and more. He knew her name, and said it gently. He was dressed impeccably, in cream twill trousers and a black silk shirt that opened to reveal a gold chain. Elements of the 70's were definitely there, but he was a 90's kind of guy. Tall. Thin. Tan, even though it was December. He reminded her of someone, but she couldn't quite remember who.

"I've never met a man quite like you," she admitted timidly. "I have to confess that I've never had a man do my hair before."

"You're in for an adventure, then," he cooed. "Have you ever thought about a more wispy look?"

Shirley frowned, unsure.

"It's more youthful."

"Go for it!"

Two hours later, Shirley had been transformed. Her hair was shorter and darker. Randall had convinced her to "go back to her roots" and color it similar to the shade nature had given her, only with highlights.

She had also indulged in a manicure, her first professional buff and shine. Randall had advised her on some new makeup tips, and Shirley was actually looking forward to a bolder shade of red.

When she drove off, she was much poorer, but she felt younger and prettier than she had in a very long time. Rita had been right. That's when it hit her. Randall reminded her of Rita!

That night when the family was all dressed and at the mall to have their family picture taken, Shirley was feeling very proud to be part of her clan. She had chosen black and white for their color scheme, and was wearing a new black outfit. She'd exchanged the ones she'd bought earlier for this one, and had to admit that black did have a thinning effect. Or maybe it was just her mind that was thinning. Either way, she felt charged, ready, and raring for the *whole* holiday experience, including mugging for the camera.

"You look pretty with makeup on, Mommy," Sara complimented her.

Stan nodded. "You should wear it more often."

"I always wear makeup." Shirley tried not to snap.

"I never saw it before," Sara replied.

Stan grinned and pursed his lips together, then pretended to zip his mouth shut.

As they walked through the mall, Shirley felt happy in spite of the crowds. "I hope the studio takes us right in," she said, "so I don't fade first."

Shirley's hopes were dashed as soon as she saw the mile-long line in front of the photo studio. At least a dozen other families, many with screaming babies, were waiting to be "shot." Turns out Stan's mother had invested two dollars and ninety-nine cents for a gift certificate that allowed them a free photo sitting. That included no photographs. Those had to be purchased separately. The "best value package" the place offered included one hundred prints of the pose of their choice. Shirley knew she didn't know that many people who would want their family photo.

"Do you have any packages that just offer three photos?"

The woman behind the counter looked as tired and worn has Shirley had that morning. "No," she answered.

"Does this remind you of anything?" Shirley asked Samantha.

Samantha frowned. "Yeah, it reminds me of standing in line with the kids so they could get their picture taken with Santa."

"Exactly."

It took nearly an hour of separating boxing children, humoring Stan, and keeping Stephen awake, before Shirley and her family got to sit in front of the camera for a total of three minutes.

"I want to stand in back," Shirley insisted. "Hide me." She tried to position everyone quickly, saving a pocket of just enough space so that her head showed, but her body did not.

"Say, 'Cheese!' " ordered the same woman who had tried to

sell them the hundred-picture package. Shirley did not have time to pose herself, let alone check her hair, before the woman pressed a small sliver button on the end of a hand-held cable.

Snap. Crackle. Pop. The tiny room exploded with light.

"Next, please!" the woman shouted.

A teenage boy, not much older than Samantha, escorted them into a tiny adjoining room with a video screen where images of their not-so-happy family flashed across a white screen.

The wisp in Shirley's hair had wilted. Stan's fly was wide open. Stephen was wailing. Sara's eyes were closed. Sean appeared like he was suffering from a serious stomachache. But Samantha looked good, and Shirley ordered a set of Christmas cards.

"Which imprint do you think we should choose, Stan—HO . . . HO . . . HO, or PEACE ON EARTH?"

He looked confused, unable to come up with an answer.

The photo package cost them *a lot* more than the advertised price. Shirley wanted to argue, but then focused on Stan's expression. The glower in his eyes screamed "DIVORCE."

"Don't you know places like this are nothing but a gimmick?" he chided her. "We should have gone to a *real* portrait studio. This is a joke."

Shirley shook her head. "Don't criticize me now. It was *your* mother who forked over the three bucks for our sitting certificate."

"That's exactly why you should have known better."

"You're right," relented Shirley. "I'm wrong. There, does that make you feel better?"

They were the last words any of them spoke for the rest of the evening.

Fourteen

Saturday morning Shirley called the hair salon and asked Randall for some tips on restyling her do.

"I mouse it, I rat it, I spray it, and it still looks like I got caught in a bad windstorm."

"Come on in; I'll do it for free," he offered.

Shirley could not refuse anything with the word *free* attached to it. Since she could not arrange for a baby-sitter on such short notice, she was forced to take Stephen along. She felt extremely self-conscious having him sit on her lap while Randall overhauled her hair, but Randall played with the baby and made Shirley feel comfortable at the same time.

"You have a real gift with people," she told him appreciatively. "Do you have children?"

"No, but I love kids," he revealed, dangling a pink sponge roller in front of Stephen's chubby little fingers.

"It shows. Are you married?"

"Nope."

Shirley grinned deviously. "How would you like to come to a Christmas party next week at my house?"

He hesitated.

She rolled her eyes and shook her head. "You aren't Jewish, are you?"

Randall chuckled. "Hardly. I'm . . . I'm . . . I'm sort of Catholic."

"Isn't that like being sort of pregnant?" she teased.

He tossed the pink roller back into a silver bin. "I see your point."

"Well, then . . . ?"

Randall shrugged. "I'd love to come to your party, Shirley. Thanks. Just let me know what you want me to bring. I make a mean shrimp dip!"

"Wow! A man who can style hair *and* cook! You're my kind of guy."

Randall scrunched his brow. "I wouldn't be so sure."

He then twirled the chair around so Shirley could see herself in the mirror. He had parted her hair on the side and combed it up into a tight twist.

"I've never worn my hair up before," she admitted, "but I like it. At least, I think I do. Don't you think it makes my face look thinner?"

"Are you fishing for compliments, Shirley? Because if you are, you look fetching."

Shirley didn't have the faintest clue what "fetching" meant.

"Fetching, huh? That's about the sexiest thing a man has ever said to me." She winked before she realized that Randall might misconstrue her flippancy as flirtation. What was wrong with her? She had never had a man deep-massage her scalp before, that's what was wrong. Or right, depending on perspective. She could feel her face burn hot and red. If he noticed, Randall gave no indication.

He reached down and picked up Stephen. He tried to get the baby to gaze at his own reflection in the mirror, but Stephen did not seem the least bit interested. Shirley, however, could not quit staring at her own "fetching" image.

She spent the remainder of the day in a whirlwind. First, to the church to help set up the Christmas carnival, then to drop Samantha off at *The Nutcracker* run-through. She had to buy a new white shirt for Sean to wear because she burned a hole in his old one with the iron. While she was shopping for Sean, she decided to purchase a new dressy outfit for Stephen; it might increase his chances in the cute-baby contest Mertyl Casper was judging. In between all of the big-day preparations, Shirley kept busy with the million and one errands that occupied her every day.

An hour before Stan was supposed to leave for Sara's school, he called to say that he would not be able to make the appointment.

"What do you mean, you *can't* make it?" she demanded in a voice that bordered on panic. "Those kids are all expecting Santa Claus."

"Curtis has set up a tele-conference meeting with the Japanese investors. He told me I *have* to be here to help explain 'his' proposal."

Shirley wanted to curse him, but could tell from the quiver in his voice that he didn't want to miss Sara's school performance. He wanted to play Santa, not Curtis's flunky.

"What can I do?" she asked weakly, trying to play the supportive wife, even though she knew she was not up for the role. Not tonight. Any other night but tonight.

"You can call Sara's school and tell them that I can't make it. Surely, they have to have a backup possibility."

They didn't. When Shirley informed Mrs. Wilcox, the teacher about burst into tears. "The children will be so disappointed."

"Isn't there anyone else who could fill in, perhaps one of the other parents? Who did you have last year?"

Now Mrs. Wilcox *did* burst into tears. "My dear husband, Chuck, has been our Santa for years. But he's . . . well, he's . . . this year he's undergone a little elective surgery, and I'm afraid his nose is temporarily caved in on one side. His appearance right now would frighten the children more than entertain them."

"I'll think of something," Shirley promised, assuring Mrs. Wilcox not to worry. Shirley was thinking of the Santa from the mall—the Pic 'n' Save lady. First she raced to the mall, but the Santa booth was now featuring a photo op with Rudolph—the *plastic* reindeer. The green elf in charge of the show was no help at all. Shirley suspected that she remembered her from the day that Sara drenched Santa's knee.

The next stop was to the Pic 'n' Save store, but it was closed for the evening.

Shirley wondered how she was ever going to be able to pull it off, but then she did something she never thought she could do—she asked for help. She called her in-laws and asked if they would be able to attend Sara's school program instead of going to *The Nutcracker* to watch Samantha.

Shirley explained her situation, then made a frantic proposal. "I've got to be at the church social for the first forty-five minutes or so, then I'll buzz over to the school and you can head to the *The Nutcracker*, since it will last at least two hours."

Shirley was grateful that her father-in-law had answered the phone, because he seemed to understand her proposal, as muffled as she presented it. "Of course we'll help you out," he told her. "If we miss Sami's performance tonight, tell her we'll be there tomorrow night."

"God bless you, Dad. You're the greatest." Shirley felt like a mountain had just been lifted from her shoulders.

She immediately strapped the weight right back on.

Shirley locked herself in the bathroom and tried on the Santa outfit that Stan had for Sara's school play. It fit—*without* the padding.

"I won't think about this now," she vowed aloud, sounding like a frumpy Scarlet O'Hara. "I'll think about it tomorrow." She had too much to do tonight. Too much to do for one woman, but not when her burden was shared.

Rita arrived right on time to pick up Sean for his recital.

"I want to go with Aunt Rita," Sara whimpered, still upset because she had overheard the confrontation between Shirley and Stan, and knew that her father would not be able to play Santa that evening.

"Don't worry, honey. Maybe the *real* Santa will stop by for a visit."

She looked at her mother skeptically, still spouting tears, but Shirley didn't have time to console her like she would have liked to.

Rita knelt down and embraced the child. "After your program at school is finished, you're going to come to Sami's play. I'll be there, and you can sit on my lap. We'll watch sugarplum fairies dance together."

"Okay," said Sara, bear-hugging Rita around her perfectly pressed dress.

Rita looked over at Shirley and mouthed: "I don't know how you do it."

"I don't," Shirley mouthed back.

Lena called to let Shirley know that everything at *The Nutcracker* run-through had gone fine. "Samantha's all dressed and ready. She's a little nervous, but wouldn't you be if you were dancing in front of hundreds of people?"

"That's a silly question, Mom."

"You're right, Shirley," agreed Lena. "I just wanted to let you know that everything here is under control Don't worry. I'll save a whole row of seats for whoever else manages to show up. Sami and I will be fine. You really ought to ask for my help a little more often. If you weren't so proud and independent, your life would run a lot smoother."

"I'm sure you're right, Mom. Thank you," Shirley said sincerely.

Stan's parents picked up Sara. They actually seemed glad that Shirley had requested their help, especially her father-in-law, whose bald head Shirley kissed with gratitude. She smiled at her mother-in-law. "Thank you both."

"I'll see you at *The Nutcracker*," Shirley assured Sara, never letting on that she would see her *before* that.

As soon as they left, Shirley bundled Stephen up and ran out the door, headed for the church social. By the time she realized she had forgotten Stephen's new outfit, and that he was wearing a stained T-shirt and baby sweats, it was too late to drive all the way back home. Maybe she would just leave him in his baby parka and tell Mertyl Casper that she'd sewn him an Eskimo costume.

Shirley stayed just long enough to greet fellow church-goers, emcee the opening program, help with the cakewalk, and watch Stephen place third in the baby contest.

"He would have placed higher, but honestly, Shirley, hon, you could have at least had him wear matching socks." Mertyl's tone sounded more baffled than accusatory. Shirley knew the poor woman was perplexed, wondering how a mother could bring her baby to a cute-kid contest dressed like Stephen was dressed.

"Third place is just fine." Shirley beamed, refusing to let Mertyl Casper's world of order clash with hers. Not tonight.

"There were only three babies entered," Mertyl snipped.

Shirley brushed past her toward the nearest exit, running head-on into Pastor Dalebout's wife, who was balancing a cake in each hand.

"I'm so sorry," Shirley apologized.

Mrs. Dalebout smiled. "No harm done, dear." Then she nodded toward Stephen, who was wadded in the crook of Shirley's arm. "That baby of yours is adorable. He would have won that contest if he'd only been awake."

Shirley swallowed. Stephen *had* been awake. Just not alert. "Merry Christmas," Shirley called, hurrying away. Maybe after the hustle of the holidays had slowed, she would take him to a specialist. Maybe there *was* a problem. Shirley shook her head, letting the cold crisp air freeze out any worries. Worries could wait.

Shirley shimmied and shook herself into the Santa suit, using her car for a changing room. She had to smile when Mertyl Casper walked across the parking lot and saw Shirley donning a beard. She waved and headed toward the car, but Shirley sped off before the woman could interrogate her.

Mrs. Wilcox met Shirley at the back door. She nodded in amazement. "I think you are the best Santa I've ever seen."

"Ho, ho, ho." Shirley shook like a bowlful of jelly. "Santa would really appreciate it if you could tend Stephen while I pay a visit to the other children."

"I'm surprised Stephen isn't crying," mused Mrs. Wilcox, adjusting Stephen on her hip. "Most babies would be terrified to see their mothers sporting a beard and talking in such a gruff voice."

"Ah, he's used to it."

Even Sara didn't recognize her own mother.

Shirley had to admit—it was a jolly good time. She smiled at her in-laws, who were seated in the audience. Her mother-in-law refused to make eye contact with Shirley, but her father-in-law asked for a second lollipop from Santa's goody bag.

As soon as Santa had given out the last treat bag, Shirley rushed in the back and changed, then she and Stephen headed to *The Nutcracker*. Everyone else was already there and seated. Even Stan had made it.

Family. Friends. Christians. Jews. All of them people Shirley loved.

"What do you think?" Stan whispered, pointing his chin toward the stage where Sami was pirouetting.

It took a long moment for Shirley to reply. "I think this is what Christmas is all about," she whispered, slipping her hand into his.

Fifteen

The final week before Christmas, Shirley felt invigorated, ready to tackle the world. Samantha still had performances scheduled, and Shirley had to get ready for Stan's office party, but the rest was a matter of one errand after another.

The first one was to play Cupid.

"Hello, Rita. It's me. I realize that you're Jewish, and so please don't let what I'm about to do offend you—but I am in charge of Stan's Christmas office party, and would really love it if you could come. Nothing religious and nothing fancy. Just a small shindig at my house."

"I'd love to come," she accepted eagerly. "But I'm not part of Stan's company."

"Doesn't matter a bit. There are always a few extra people to liven things up a bit. Besides, it was Stan's idea to invite you. He think you'll add a snazzy new dimension to the ordinary crowd."

"Really?" Rita sounded surprised. "I didn't think Stan cared for me."

"Why would you say that? Stan likes you a lot. He thinks you bring out the best in me."

"I didn't realize that. I thought he felt I was intruding in your life too much."

"Not at all. He's glad that I have a friend like you who rockets me out of my comfort zone every once in a while. You've taught me a lot in just a short time."

"Thanks, Shirley. I'd love to come. When is your party?"

"Thursday night about six o'clock. You don't need to bring anything, and remember, nothing gets religious. It's just a chance for everyone to get together and socialize."

Shirley was making the whole affair sound a lot more positive than she actually felt about it. She still resented the way she and Stan had been bamboozled by Curtis, but she was determined to not let the creep dampen their holidays. Now that most of the pressure had lifted, Shirley felt ready to play the supportive wife again.

"It sounds like a lot of fun," said Rita. "Thanks for inviting me. I'll talk to you before Thursday to check on all of the details."

Shirley didn't dare mention that the real reason she wanted Rita to come was so she could line her up with Randall. Same basic age. Both were a little eclectic and dressed like fashion-magazine models. Shirley was sure something good would come of it.

The next thing to do on Shirley's dwindling list was to finally buy a blue Monster Mountain Masher for Sean. That she knew she could pick up anywhere from the grocery store to the mall. They were everywhere. And she had thought of a place to hide it that Sean would never guess—under his *own* bed. That was the one place no one dared to look, especially Sean. Too many moldy treasures were stashed under there, everything from lost homework to half-eaten donuts. Every once in a while, Shirley raked it out, but there were only a few days left until Christmas, and so she felt that was the safest hiding place.

The only problem turned out to be that the piles of Monster Mountain Mashers were gone. No blues ones. No red ones. No black ones. No green ones. No Monster Mountain Mashers to be found.

Shirley checked the grocery store. The mall. The department stores. The drugstore. The pet store.

"What happened to the millions of Monster Mountain Mashers?" she asked the clerk at the hardware store.

"I'm not sure. It must have been all the TV advertising the company started doing. Those toys were piled in here for a month just collecting dust, then all of a sudden people were lined up to buy them. Our stock flew out of here like crazy."

"Well, I need you to order me a blue one and have it here before Christmas," she stated with force.

The man laughed at her. "Lady, there's no way. We might get another shipment of the things sometime in January."

"January! But Christmas is at the end of this week. That's the only thing my son has asked for for the past month."

The man shrugged his shoulders. "You should have bought one, then."

Shirley felt sick inside. She called Stan and told him the problem.

"Why didn't you buy one before now?" he asked.

"Don't blame me for this," she snapped. "If you were involved in this holiday at all, I might not have had a nervous breakdown, and forgotten to buy our son the only thing he wanted!"

"Well, I'll go right after work and see if I can find a red one."

"*Blue*, Stanley. A blue one. But take whatever you can get at this point."

She didn't mean to be so edgy, but she was panicked, and she knew she only had herself to blame.

As she turned to drive into her neighborhood, two cars were parked smack in the middle of the road, blocking her driveway. The drivers were engaged in friendly chitchat. Shirley, annoyed beyond reason, blasted her horn and pulled up alongside the nearest car. Who were these jerks, and didn't they know it was dangerous to block the road, just so they could gab? Shirley rolled down the window and screamed a blue streak of obscenities at the driver.

The shocked woman driver whirled around and . . . smiled at Shirley.

It was Pastor Dalebout's wife.

Shirley squeezed her eyes shut, desperately wanting to crawl under her seat—to disintegrate.

"Hello, Shirley," the pastor's wife said deliberately. "I'm so sorry . . . sorry we were blocking the road. I was just at your house dropping off a plate of home-baked goodies when I recognized an old friend of mine. We shouldn't have stopped in the road like we did. You're right, we were idiotic. I'm so sorry," she sputtered. "I made the brownies with pecans and whipped frosting, just the way you like them. The pastor and I wanted to thank you for all of your work on the Christmas social. You did a great job."

The accosted woman sped away before Shirley could lift her jaw to respond. The other driver turned out to be Shirley's newest neighbor, who had driven off as soon as Shirley first opened her mouth.

Shirley wanted to die of embarrassment. She told herself she *should* die of embarrassment. Instead, she went right home and fought the kids for the last three pecan brownies.

Sixteen

It was no use. Every Monster Mountain Masher ever made was already sold. Millions were no doubt gift-wrapped, waiting to be delivered on Christmas morning to anxious children who had requested them. Shirley cursed the effectiveness of TV advertising.

How could she have known? Shirley spent two precious days of her final week before Christmas traipsing around the city and even surrounding towns, desperately searching for Sean's requested Christmas present. Rita even checked the Internet. No use.

"Maybe he'll settle for Rollerblades," she suggested to Stan.

Stan shook his head. "I already asked him. I even tempted him with a puppy. No good. He's sure he's getting a blue Monster Mountain Masher since he asked for it so early."

"Don't look at me like that," she warned her husband. "I feel rotten about this. I—"

Stan touched her softly on the cheek. "Don't worry about it. Sean will understand. We can get him a blue one *and* a red one in January."

Shirley felt her eyes fill with tears. "I really screwed up this time."

Stan did his best to console Shirley. It didn't work because she wasn't feeling sorry for herself.

"I feel sorry for Sean," she said. "He's been a great kid all year, and the only thing he asks for is one lousy toy for Christmas, and I fail him."

The futile search for the elusive Monster Mountain Masher sucked the Christmas spirit right out of Shirley. She went through the motions, but the closer they got to December 25, the less Shirley felt like celebrating.

She finished shopping, except for the one gift she could not find to buy. She worked together with the office wives and a few of their husbands to organize the Christmas party. She scrubbed the house at night and even cleaned out the refrigerator. She addressed the remainder of her Christmas cards and sent them out at the last minute. She wrapped boxes, tied ribbons, made eggnog, and played the Carpenters' Christmas album a dozen times.

She attended every one of Samantha's *Nutcracker* performances. At night she read to the children. But in the back of her mind loomed that blue Monster Mountain Masher.

Shirley also took two more loads of presents to the women's shelter. Instead of lifting her, the experience depressed her. She felt guilty for feeling so bad about something as insignificant as a Monster Mountain Masher, when there were children without love, food, and shelter. But Sean was one little boy who was very significant to Shirley, and his feelings mattered to her more than her own ever would.

The kids got out of school for the holiday on December 23, the same day as the party. It was also the last performance of Sami's *Nutcracker*. Once again, the grandparents came to the rescue, attending, so that Shirley and Stan could play host and hostess to Curtis and his cronies.

"I actually do like a lot of the people I work with," said Stan. "I just can't stand my boss."

"Relax," replied Shirley, "the food is all ready. The house is clean and the party is going to be great. The office is closed, and you've got the whole day off. Don't even think about Curtis."

Stan frowned. "It's not that easy. You don't know what he's done now."

Shirley inhaled and braced herself. "What?"

"He's got a couple of important investors from Japan flying into town tomorrow. I'm suppose to pick them up from the airport and see that they are taken care of while they are here."

"But tomorrow is Christmas Eve!"

"I know," he said. "There is nothing I can do about it, except quit my job."

Shirley was not angry with Stan, but she was livid with Curtis. She just couldn't take it out on Curtis, so she grunted her disapproval and stomped out of the room like an angry preschooler.

She could feel her usual burden of guilt weigh even heavier. She'd disappointed her son, her daughter, and just vented unfairly at her husband. Shirley wasn't sure what was *really* pressuring her, but she felt like a volcano about to blow.

The rest of the day was spent preparing for the party. Stan volunteered to help any way he could, so Shirley sent him out shopping with the kids.

"When Daddy asks what I want for Christmas, tell him CASH," Shirley coached her children. "In unmarked bills."

They promised to stay away and out of Shirley's hair for at least a few hours. They had only been gone a few minutes when the telephone rang.

"I am calling for Stanley," a *very* unfamiliar male voice said. "Is he there?"

"I'm sorry, he's not," Shirley replied. "Can I help you? I'm his wife."

"I am Akihiro Tumate from Japan. I am at airport with business companion. We need ride."

"Stan is not available. I know he thought you were not arriving until tomorrow."

"We are here now. Today." The way the man spoke reminded Shirley of chopping vegetables. Sharp, hard, single syllables.

"I'm sure someone at the office is available to pick you up," said Shirley, slowly realizing that no one was available. The office was closed for the day.

Shirley swore under her breath. Taming her profanity would be another one of her new year's resolutions. Until then, she was going to make the most of her current vice.

She quizzed Tumate until she had managed to get his flight number and location.

"Stay there. It will take me about an hour to drive to the airport, but I'll pick you up myself."

Shirley quickly changed Stephen into a dry diaper, gave herself a sponge bath, and put on her new Fantasy bra and her black pantsuit. She knew that by the time she got back from the airport, it would be time for the party to start. She was halfway across town when she realized she had forgotten to leave Stan a note telling him where she went and why. Someone should have told Santa that what this family really needed was a cell phone.

Traffic was fierce, and no driver on the road showed any sign of having the Christmas spirit, though the unavoidable driver in front of Shirley seemed to have already drunk more than his share of holiday "spirits."

By the time Shirley found a parking place at the airport, she was was thirty minutes late. She grabbed Stephen, and rushed through the crowded airport to find Gate D, where the foreign visitors were no doubt wondering if they were going to have to walk. *I should have insisted they take a taxi,* she thought, too late.

Shirley sat her purse on the belt at the security station and hurried underneath the metal arch. Immediately, an alarm screamed. Shirley never suspected that she was the culprit.

"Excuse me, ma'am, but would you please step this way?" a six-foot-seven, 310-pound security officer asked her.

"Okay," said Shirley, "but I'm in a hurry. I put my purse on the belt and you checked it out."

"It's not your *purse* that concerns us. It's your *person*. Would you please hand me the baby and walk under the arch one more time, very slowly."

Shirley handed Stephen to the officer and stepped under the security arch.

BUZZZZZZ!

"Ma'am, are you carrying any metal object on your person?" the officer inquired, handing Stephen back to Shirley.

"No. Something must be wrong with your machine. Like I said, I'm in a hurry. I have to pick up some men for my husband's company. They don't speak much English, and I'm afraid they'll be confused. Besides, look behind me at all of those people we are holding up. They are going to miss their flights."

"Ma'am, please step this way," said another officer, just as big and just as unfriendly-looking.

With Stephen squirming in her arms, Shirley stood immobile, wondering how on earth anyone could think she might be a security risk.

Two uniformed women suddenly appeared with an instrument resembling a silver wand and moved it slowly up and down Shirley's body while at least two hundred total strangers gawked.

"I haven't had this much attention in years." She made a feeble attempt at terse humor. The incident reminded her of the security search fiasco Diana Ross had once encountered in London. "I'm not even a celebrity," Shirley muttered.

No response.

The wand elicited an ugly beep and pulsating light whenever it passed over a certain part of Shirley's anatomy.

"Are you wearing an underwire bra, by any chance?" one of the security officers questioned.

Shirley felt her her face flush red. She knew she was wearing enough wire to fence in a cattle herd. "Do I have to take it off?"

"That won't be necessary, ma'am. Please, step this way," another officer directed her across the corridor to the ladies' room.

"Thanks," Shirley whispered hoarsely. "I can assure you this is all totally unnecessary. I am no national security risk. None whatsoever."

The team of experts ignored her, but it seemed to Shirley that they took more time than necessary to complete their job before releasing her.

"Sorry for the inconvenience," said one officer. "Merry Christmas."

Shirley grabbed Stephen, rushed down the corridor, stopped, looked back, and rumbled, "Bah, humbug!"

It was nearly time for the party to start before Shirley discovered two lone Japanese businessmen enjoying a Bud Lite in the airport bar. Akihiro and Fumi were pleasant enough. It was Shirley who felt frazzled. She did, however, manage to call Stan from a pay phone to let him know where she was, and why she had been detained.

He laughed. And laughed and laughed.

Shirley took her time driving home, actually enjoying the company of the foreign visitors. They were Buddhists, but still showed a great deal of interest in the American observance of Christmas.

"Who is this Jesus Christ," Fumi asked, "the one for whom you celebrate?"

Shirley paused. The directness of the question caught her unprepared. No one had ever asked her that before. "He was the son of God," she answered carefully.

"And who is *your* God?" Akihiro questioned.

The ride home turned into a question-and-question period. Shirley answered the best she could, but the inquiries they posed gave Shirley cause to contemplate her own fluctuating faith. Maybe that's why she could relate to Rita so well. It was at least one thing the two women had in common.

Stan had the party fairly well under control by the time they arrived home. Samantha was at *The Nutcracker* with her grandparents. Sean and Sara were at the neighbor's being baby-sat. Most of the guests had arrived. Shirley quickly introduced Akihiro and Fumi to Stan, and then let him take over while she went to freshen up.

Randall had arrived and was standing in the corner, drinking eggnog. He was dressed in an olive linen suit and a black turtleneck. He looked more like a movie star than her hairstylist. The man had presence, Shirley had to give him that. She hugged him, introduced him to Stan, then promised to return right after she put the baby down and did some quick touch-ups to her hair and face.

When she returned, Shirley was surprised to find Randall in apparently deep conversation with Curtis. He, too, was wearing a linen suit, even though his memo had stated that dress was supposed to be casual. The two men seemed to be getting acquainted.

Good thing, because the doorbell rang and Stan announced Rita's arrival. She looked very uneasy, but elegant. She was dressed in a red dress with a gold belt that showed off her twenty-four-inch waist. Her hair was styled perfectly, her makeup flawless. She didn't mean to, but just her presence made Shirley feel like the average overweight American housewife.

Shirley tried to forget her own insecurities, to remember why she had invited Rita. "Thanks for coming. I'm sure this isn't the kind of party you're used to, but I'm glad you're here."

"I'm glad to be here," said Rita. "It's the only party I've attended all season."

"Don't Jews have parties to celebrate Hanukkah?"

"Yes. I just haven't attended any this year. I thought of having your family celebrate Hanukkah with me this year. Fun games and great food are involved, but I just couldn't do it this year. Maybe next year."

Shirley smiled, glad to know that even Rita couldn't do

everything. "Just the thought means a lot. Next year you help me do Christmas and I'll help you do Hanukkah. Deal?"

Rita laughed. "Deal."

Shirley introduced her around the room. When she got to Randall, Shirley watched carefully, hoping for sparks.

There were none. Shirley pressed, telling each one more and more about the other. She informed them of all they had in common.

They were both from the West Coast, Randall from California, Rita from Washington state. They were both career people. Very artistic. Kind. Thoughtful. Skilled. Well-adorned and, most important, *single*.

Not even a flicker.

Shirley was disappointed, but tried not to show it. Randall returned to his conversation with Curtis, while Rita struck up a three-way with the Japanese businessmen.

Shirley overheard Rita tell them about her travels to various parts of Japan. Shirley was really impressed when she heard Rita even speak some Japanese to the men.

"Your friend Rita is really something," said Stan, sounding grateful. "Normally, Japanese men find it challenging to discuss business with women, but Rita seems to have them enthralled."

"I wish she could catch Randall's eye."

"No luck, huh?"

"Struck out," she had to admit. "I can't figure out why. Those two could be twins."

There was plenty of food and beverages, but Shirley felt the party lagging.

Stan put his arm around Shirley and whispered, "What can we do to liven things up a bit?"

"Tell some jokes," she suggested.

He cleared his throat nervously. "Have you heard the one about kids and Christmas?" he shouted needlessly, since no one was talking above a whisper, and most people weren't talking at all.

"You know, kids don't believe in things like the Easter Bunny," Stan continued, "or Santa Claus anymore. Why, just mention the Tooth Fairy and kids think you're talking about some dentist in San Francisco!"

Shirley smirked.

She was the *only* one. For the next twenty seconds, the room fell dead silent.

Then Randall laughed, a hearty laugh that allowed everyone else to resume breathing. Shirley winked at him gratefully.

It took a few minutes before private conversations struck up again. Rita helped Shirley arrange shrimp on the trays.

"I realize the joke was dumb, but don't you people act a little weird?" Shirley whispered.

Rita narrowed her eyes and looked at her, firmly, steadily. "Not really."

Shirley was going to ask Rita what she meant by that, but Stan came up and uncorked a fresh bottle of zinfandel.

"So much for my humor," he said. "Was it my timing?"

Rita curved her lips, but remained rigid. "I don't think so."

Shirley popped a shrimp covered in cocktail sauce into Stan's open mouth. "Thank goodness for Randall. He's a sport."

Rita laughed easily at that comment.

Stan turned to Rita. "I guess you've figured out that Shirley was playing matchmaker here tonight. What do you think of Randall?"

"I think he *is* a sport," Rita answered. "A very good one at that."

"Have you noticed how much attention he is giving Curtis?" asked Stan. "I wonder if they are talking about Curtis's haircut."

Rita looked knowingly at Shirley, then nodded for Stan to observe his boss a little more astutely. "Maybe Randall and Curtis have more in common than you realize," she said it slowly, as if saying it too fast would confuse both Stan and Shirley.

Shirley looked at Stan.

Stan looked at Shirley.

They both looked at Rita, then at the two men conversing in the corner of the room.

Slowly, but surely, it dawned on them why no one had laughed at Stan's joke.

It wasn't funny.

Seventeen

At the first opportunity, Shirley apologized to Randall. "I'm so sorry if I offended you. My husband didn't mean anything by that joke."

Randall laughed good-naturedly. "I don't take offense. I've had fun, and I'm glad I got acquainted with some new people."

Shirley knew he wasn't talking about Rita.

She watched for the rest of the night, but Stan and Curtis did not exchange a single word. She told herself that knowing Curtis, Stan just might receive a pink slip for a Christmas bonus this year.

Rita spent much of the evening putting the Japanese visitors at ease. They explored the house, commenting on all of the festive decorations. Shirley had no idea what they were saying, but she liked the way they pointed at the decorations and nodded.

"Way to go, Cupid!" Rita teased Shirley, once they were alone in the kitchen. "You'd better leave my love life to more observant matchmakers—maybe those telephone physics."

Shirley laughed freely. Except for the fact that Stan might be out of a job any day now, most of the pressure of the season was gone. She still felt horrid about the Monster Mountain Masher, but Shirley felt pretty good about the majority of the other things that had transpired during the past month.

She visited with Rita, who stayed to help her clean up after everyone else left. Rita watched Stephen while Shirley ran next door to pick up a sleepy Sean and Sara. Stan had gone to get the tired, but gracious, Japanese businessmen settled into their downtown hotel.

Rita left shortly after Stan's parents brought Samantha home, exhausted but excited about her final performance in *The Nutcracker*.

"I'm so sorry I couldn't be there," Shirley heard herself

apologizing once again that night. "It seems like I'm always saying 'I'm sorry,' but, Sami, I really am. I wanted to be there for your closing performance."

"Don't sweat it, Mom. You were there every other night. Besides, you don't have to be there, to be there, if you know what I mean. I could feel you there."

Shirley felt tears burn her eyes. She knew Samantha hated it when she cried. "I'm very proud of you, sweetheart."

"Next year just make sure you keep your holiday schedule free," said Samantha, hugging her mother.

"Next year?" Shirley didn't even want to entertain the thought.

"Yeah, next year I'm trying out for *The Swan Princess*!"

"Good luck," said her mother.

"You don't mean that," replied Sami, stuffing a leftover shrimp into her mouth.

Sami was right, she didn't mean it, but she would when the time came.

"Maybe next year we'll just skip Christmas," Shirley suggested. "Now, how would you like to help your old decrepit mother finish cleaning up?"

Samantha looked wounded. "I would, Mom, but I think I'm coming down with a flu bug." She coughed and slapped her hand against her forehead.

Shirley played along. She felt Samantha's forehead and pulled back, shaking her hand as if she had just touched a hot stove. "Good night, my scorching sugarplum fairy."

Later, while lying in bed, Shirley scratched Stan's back.

"Why are you being so nice?" he asked suspiciously.

"Because now that things are settling down, I am feeling a little less harried, and a little more grateful."

"Do you think I'll still have a job when Christmas is over?" he asked seriously.

For a while they talked about his job, his boss, his frustrations. Then they talked about her job, how she liked being her own boss, and her frustrations.

"No more of this trivial stuff," she said, "I've got a weighty question for you."

"Now what?"

"What's Christmas all about?"

"What do you mean?"

"I mean *why* do we celebrate Christmas?" Shirley asked.

"Is this another one of your trick questions?"

"No, I'm serious."

He waited before answering. "To show how much we care for one another. To share goodwill that doesn't exist throughout most of the year."

Shirley shifted her pillow into a more comfortable position. "Exactly—but you're missing my point. *Why* do we have Christmas in the first place? What is it really all about?"

"What is *what* all about?"

"Christmas is supposed to commemorate the birth of Jesus Christ, right?"

He looked clueless, and too tired to delve into such depths with her tonight. "Right."

"Well . . . was Jesus Christ real?"

Stan sat up in bed. "What do you mean, 'Was he real?' "

"I mean did he *really* exist, and if he did, was he who he said he was, or was Jesus just a very good man and a master teacher?"

"Shirley, you know that Jesus Christ was the Son of God. You know that. Why all the questions?"

"Because my faith fluctuates lately. Akihiro and Fumi asked me about Jesus Christ. I had to answer them from my heart, but it made me stop and wonder."

"There's nothing wrong with that."

"But Rita lives the kind of caring, loving, serving Christian life that I'd like to be living, that I *should* be living. She doesn't believe that Christ was anything more than a mortal man."

"So? You're not Jewish, Shirley." He sounded almost disgusted. "You're not even Catholic, although I've had to remind you of that a few times in the past, because you're so fond of all the ceremonies and the formalities."

"And I'm not our neighbor Mrs. Gleed either."

Stan groaned. "*Now* what are you talking about?"

"In my opinion, Mrs. Gleed is what a Christian should be. She is always doing for others and improving herself along the way." Shirley told him all about her "apron visit."

"Nellie Gleed is someone very special," Stan agreed. "Is there any of her fudge left?"

"Not a bite!" Shirley rubbed his shoulders. "Someday I'm

going to study all of the religions of the world to make sure that I'm living the right teachings."

"Don't be so hard on yourself, Shirley. Don't compare yourself to other people. You're not Rita. You're not Mrs. Gleed. You're just Shirley."

"Just Shirley, huh?"

"Yup. And, Shirley, that is more woman than I can handle most of the time." He put his arms around her and pulled her close.

"You seem to handle me just fine," she replied, cuddling closer to him. "I'm sorry if I've been a beast this year. I just wanted Christmas to be perfect."

"It will be," he assured her. "It will be the best Christmas ever."

Shirley lay quietly for a long time, long enough for Stan's rhythmic breathing to assure her he was asleep. Her mind had wandered two thousand years back to a little town called Bethlehem.

Then Shirley spoke to the darkness. "This won't be the best Christmas ever, no matter what happens—the best Christmas ever was the very *first* Christmas."

Eighteen

On Christmas Eve, Shirley made a last-ditch effort to locate Sean's blue Monster Mountain Masher. No luck. She came home crestfallen and wrapped a dozen other trivial gifts addressed to him. It was a futile attempt to appease her guilt—to prove to her son that he had not been forsaken.

Then it was time for a repeat of Thanksgiving dinner—sans the turkey and homemade rolls. She popped the frozen lasagna into the oven and checked to see if the frozen roll dough was starting to thaw. She'd forgotten to set it out earlier. Oh, well, her mother-in-law might really have something to complain about tonight. She didn't care. She didn't have the time or the energy left to care.

"Will you help me get dinner ready for your grandparents?" Shirley asked Samantha, who was at the table painting her nails.

"I would, but I'm feeling a little nauseous," she said. "I think I wore myself out with all the running back and forth to *The Nutcracker* practices."

Shirley smirked. "I know what you mean. Now go get the soup out of the fridge and put it on the stove. Then help me set the table."

"Why do you always do this, Mom? You invite people over so we can't ever just relax and enjoy a holiday by ourselves."

"Now you sound like your father. Christmas is a time for family and loved ones to be together. Besides, I owe your grandparents, and so do you. They really came through for us when we needed them."

Sean walked into the room and stole a carrot from the pile that Shirley was chopping for a salad. "Are we going to act out the Christmas story tonight like we always do?"

"Sure," said Shirley. "You can be Joseph."

"I'm always Joseph," he grumbled. "If I had my blue Monster Mountain Masher I could drive the Wise Men to Bethlehem in a hurry. I'd crush that old Herod."

Shirley felt her heart rip. "This year will be extra-special because we'll have a real baby Jesus." She tried to deter his train of thinking. "Stephen can lie in the laundry basket we use for the manger."

"Yeah," piped Sara. "He'll lie there and not make a fuss, just like the real baby Jesus."

Shirley felt another tear at her heart.

"I don't want to be in the play this year," Samantha announced, blowing her fingernails dry. "But I will direct it. I learned a lot about directing when I *starred* in *The Nutcracker*."

Shirley pretended not to notice Sami's pompous tone. "Sounds good to me. Now help me get ready."

"I would, but I'm getting a headache. I think I might have breathed in too many fumes from the nail polish. I'm feeling a little dizzy."

Sara, who was underneath the table wrapping surprise presents for everyone, popped out. "Mommy, what color are our pajamas going to be this year?"

"They'll be red like always," answered Sean, munching more chopped carrots. "Every year Mom sews us red pj's; this year isn't going to be different, is it, Mom?"

Shirley just stood there. How could she have forgotten one of her most vigilant holiday traditions? Even though she was no seamstress, no Mertyl Casper, once a year, Shirley made her best effort to assemble matching Christmas pajamas for the children. Somehow, in the hullabaloo of this year's schedule, that treasured tradition had never even made it to her list of things to do.

Shirley turned the kitchen duties over to a whining Samantha, and Shirley ran downtown to buy a bolt of red flannel. The fabric store was sold out. They were also sold out of green and plaid and any other material reminiscent of Christmas. There was no time to shop elsewhere, so Shirley bought a bolt of flannel material with teddy bears printed on it. Sara would love it. Stephen wouldn't have a clue, but the older kids would hate it.

So what? She could not let this tradition falter. She knew a lot of women who could actually make a buttonhole, but Shirley wasn't about to impose on someone else on Christmas Eve.

She made it back home and had time to cut out the material before she had to get dressed for Christmas Eve dinner.

Stan's parents arrived first. They bought a box of brightly-wrapped gifts to put underneath the tree.

"But you already bought that portrait gift certificate for us," Shirley pointed out.

"That was nothing," said her father-in-law.

"You've got that right," Shirley muttered under her breath.

He pecked her on the cheek as she took his coat. "I do hope it got us a photo of your family. We're so very proud of ya'll."

"It did," said Sean. "And we all look like we're mad."

"I can't wait to see it," he chuckled, tousling Sean's hair.

"Did you wear black?" her mother-in-law queried Shirley.

"Yes, Mom, I did, but I can't guarantee it did the trick."

"I suspect not," the woman grunted, eyeing Shirley from head to toe.

Shirley wondered why Stan was still in the bathroom. The thought fled through her mind that he seemed to spend an inordinate amount of time in the bathroom whenever his parents were visiting. She was wishing she had a place to hide as she escorted her in-laws into the family room.

"We bought a portrait for you and Dad, but it's wrapped underneath the tree," Shirley explained.

"We can wait," said her mother-in-law. "Tell me, what can I do to help with dinner? Dad's about starved to death."

Shirley glanced at her father-in-law. He didn't look starved. He looked totally engrossed in the Nintendo game he was playing with Sean.

"Nothing, Mom. I don't need any help from you tonight. Between the freezer and the microwave, I've got everything under control."

Lena arrived just in time to prevent an all-out war. Was it just Shirley, or did her mother-in-law's moods swing like a pendulum?

Lena came, bearing gifts—boxes of shiny gold Christmas-tree ornaments.

"Geez, Mom, did you get a good deal on these, or what?" Shirley chortled, trying to balance the stack of ornament boxes Lena shoved at her.

"What are you talking about, Shirley?"

Shirley pointed with her chin. The boxes were plastered with giant orange stickers labeled SEVENTY-FIVE PERCENT OFF.

"It's not the price, it's the thought that counts. All I was thinking is that next year you can have a tree that matches,"

"Our decorations are eclectic, Mom. Each one is meaningful. Besides, one of our trees is more your style."

"Whatever," Lena replied, her spiked heels clicking toward the kitchen.

While Shirley was stacking the ornament boxes on the top shelf of the coat closet, she wondered how she had managed to alienate both her mother-in-law and mother within the first five minutes of Christmas Eve.

Once she gathered her composure, Shirley went back into the kitchen, where she found Lena poking a fork into the lasagna.

"Thanks for the ornaments, Mom. They're beautiful."

"They're shiny. Shiny ornaments make a tree look elegant."

Shirley knew her mother would never understand that *elegant* wasn't Shirley's goal or her style. She decided that it wasn't worth the argument to try to make her mother understand why Shirley's ornaments, especially the handmade ones, were always going to outshine the store-bought ones.

"I think this lasagna is still frozen, Shirley. Did you get it from the store, or is it one that was left over from when your pastor's wife cooked right after Stephen was born?"

Shirley sighed. "Stephen is more than six months old, Mom. This lasagna is fresh. I bought it from the store last week."

Shirley had invited Rita to their family get-together, but she had graciously declined. Rita was pulling late-night duty at the shelter. She wanted Pat to have the night off so that Pat could be with her own family. Rita had not mentioned Hanukkah again, nor had they talked about Christmas or religion—just the safe and day-to-day stuff. They had, however, concluded their last conversation with season's greetings.

"Merry Christmas!" Rita said, laughing.

"Shalom!" Shirley replied cluelessly, but enthusiastically.

Mrs. Gleed, likewise, had declined. She had joined her own family somewhere in Colorado to do some snow skiing. She promised Shirley that she would bring back photos to show how she was maneuvering "those bumpy moguls."

* * *

"Where is Daddy?" Sara asked, just as Shirley was getting ready to toss the salad. "He's been gone for a long time."

"I think he's upstairs in the bathroom, sweetie."

"No, he's not," Samantha informed them, "he's with Sean."

Shirley glanced into the family room. Sean was no longer playing Nintendo with his grandfather. Lena was now manning Sean's paddle.

"Where are they?" Shirley asked, sounding confused.

"Dad took him to do some last-minute shopping. Don't worry, they won't be gone much longer, because all of the stores close early tonight."

Shirley didn't know whether to be worried or angry. Stan had left her, after all, to fend for herself among both of their mothers. But she knew he'd never fall for that argument, because it was Shirley who had issued the invitation to both women. She wondered what Stan was really up to, especially since he had taken Sean with him. Her heart pounded. Maybe . . . just maybe . . . Stan had found a blue Monster Mountain Masher. But then why had he taken Sean with him? No scenario made sense.

Shirley served olives, cheese, and other simple hors d'oeuvres until Stanley finally walked through the door with Sean.

They looked half frozen.

"Where have you been?" Shirley demanded.

"Come see," Stan motioned for Shirley and the rest of the family to join him outside in the cold and darkness.

She was genuinely perplexed, but followed, her arm wrapped around Stan's waist.

Stan waited until everyone was lined up outside, like shivering tin shoulders, before he yelled to Sean, "Hit it!"

Sean flipped a switch and the entire house lit up. Tiny sliver sparkling Christmas lights were strung along the roof and down the sides of the house. Every dormer window was perfectly lined with twinkling lights.

Shirley's head slumped against her husband's shoulder. She wiped her teary eyes on Stan's jacket.

"How on earth did you do all of this without me knowing?" she asked, her voice cracking with emotion.

"We've been working on it, little by little. I thought for sure you'd notice, but when you were too preoccupied with everything else, we decided to keep going, hoping it would turn into a surprise."

Shirley's tears were beginning to freeze on her cheeks. "Well, it did. This is the best Christmas present you could have given me." She kissed him right on the mouth.

"Now let's go back inside," he said, "I'm freezing."

As the family sat around the dinner table, enjoying the meal, Shirley thought about Thanksgiving night, and how everyone had gone around the table, naming something for which they were grateful. At that moment, Shirley looked at each person, and thought of reasons to be grateful for each one of them.

When dinner was over, the kids wrapped towels around their heads, doned old bathrobes, used perfume for myrrh, spray-painted charcoal briquettes for gold, and Shirley's bath beads for frankincense. Under Samantha's directorial debut, they acted out the Christmas story in high fashion.

This year Samantha had Stan's father play the angel Gabriel, while Stan's mother narrated. Casting Lena as the innkeeper proved genius. As usual, Shirley and Stan played barnyard animals. Shirley made a convincing cow.

"Holy cow," Stan mooed at her.

"Funny. Very funny."

When it was all over, the guests happily departed, Shirley and family engaged in some private traditions that were for immediate family only. First, they put out a plate of oatmeal and chocolate-chip cookies for Santa—plus a big glass of fresh, cold milk. Next, everyone brushed their teeth and slipped into pajamas. Then mother and children pounced on the bed, jostling for the best position.

"Can I join you tonight?" Stan asked, sprawling himself across the foot of the bed. "I love to hear these stories, too."

"You're always welcome at the foot of my bed, Stanley," she teased him. She was still very touched by the lights on the house. Never mind that on her second inspection of the masterpiece, she had noticed that some of the lights Stan had used were more than a decade old, and not all of the bulbs worked. That didn't matter. Her mother had been right—it was the thought that counted. No matter what other gifts she received for years to come, Stan's offering of lights would always be one of Shirley's most cherished Christmas presents.

They only managed to read through half of *The Christmas Miracle of Jonathan Toomey* before everyone fell soundly asleep.

The ringing telephone woke Shirley with a start. She grabbed it. "Hello."

"Hi, Shirley. It's Rita. I'm sorry to bother you on Christmas Eve, but I'm here at the shelter. We're going to need some people to help feed Christmas dinner to the city's homeless tomorrow around eleven a.m. Would you and your whole family like to come?"

Shirley nudged Stan awake and asked him.

"Sure. Sounds like a good idea," he replied, still half asleep.

"We'll be there," said Shirley. "Thanks for thinking of us."

Shirley was nearly back asleep when she remembered the pajamas! She raced out of bed and into the family room, where she began sewing. Adrenaline and Santa's cookies with a Pepsi instead of the milk kept her going for quite a while, but by the time she was down to the finish work, Shirley was using a hot glue gun, and finally a stapler, to finish those blasted Christmas pajamas.

"What are you doing?" Stan's voice startled Shirley.

"Sewing matching pajamas for the children."

"Oh," he said. "I've got to help Santa put a bike together, and to assemble a few other toys."

"One of them doesn't happen to be a blue Monster Mountain Masher, does it?"

"Sorry."

Stan walked over to Shirley and put his arms around her. "Meet me underneath the mistletoe later, and I'll give you your *real* Christmas present."

She turned to him and yawned. "It's a date."

Nineteen

"Wake up, Mommy!" yelled Sara right in Shirley's ear.

"What time is it?" Shirley muttered groggily.

"It's Christmastime!" the young girl blared. "Come on. Let's open presents!"

"Where's Daddy?" Shirley asked, hoping for an excuse to sleep a little longer.

"He's in the family room with Sean. They're playing with Sean's new Monster Mountain Masher. It's awesome!"

"What?" Shirley shot out of bed, thundered down the stairs, and raced into the family room.

There sat Stan and Sean, in front of the fireplace, both beaming as Sean crushed crumpled wrapping paper with his brand-new blue Monster Mountain Masher.

Shirley silently cursed Stan, then shot him a look that pleaded: "*Why* . . . why didn't you tell me that you found one? *How* could you have let me suffer like I did, with worry and guilt?" She cursed him again, only this time, not so silently.

Stan looked up at her. He shrugged his shoulders in puzzlement. She knew right away, the toy had not come from him.

Where, then? Who, then?

Samantha and Sara both swore they had no idea. Of course, Sara insisted that it came from Santa, handmade by North Polian elves, and to speculate in any other direction was crazy.

Shirley had never felt the wonder of Christmas like she did at that moment. She realized there had to be a logical explanation, but for as long as it lasted, Shirley believed in miracles.

What had taken weeks to plan and prepare was destroyed in a matter of minutes. Shirley tried to orchestrate the opening of the presents, but it was no use. Beautiful wrapping paper was shredded. Hard-to-find boxes were smashed. Tags discarded. Ornaments trampled. The whole process reminded Shirley of sharks at a feeding frenzy. She did insist, however, that the children be extra careful with her special gift to them—the teddy bear pajamas. Much to their chagrin, she insisted that they wear the carefully-crafted pj's, then she lined all four of the children in front of the fireplace so she could take a photo.

"It's for the family scrapbook that I'm going to make next year."

"My pajamas don't fit," Sean complained.

"Neither do mine," Sami whispered. "One of my pajama legs is a whole lot shorter than the other one. But don't gripe, you'll make Mom feel bad."

"Ouch!" cried Sara, yanking at her sleeve. "There's a staple in my pajamas!"

Stephen suddenly let out a fierce wail. Stan picked him up and pulled out a giant straight pin from the seat of his teddy bear drawers.

Everyone looked at Shirley.

"Smile!" she instructed, figuring, from the expressions of angst of all of their faces, that this photo would no doubt end up right next to their scowling family portrait.

Shirley looked around at the mess and felt guilty. Not because of the mess, but because of the abundance. Her children were spoiled rotten, and she had no one else to blame but herself.

Samantha got clothes, makeup, and music. She was happy. "I love this denim vest," she said. "It looks just like my other ones."

Sean got Rollerblades, clothes, a football, a basketball, *and* his blue Monster Mountain Masher. He was ecstatic.

Sara got clothes and a baby doll whose thumb stuck in its mouth.

"It's just what I asked Santa for!" she squealed. She also received a pink bicycle.

Stephen received a new outfit, the one that had been intended for the baby contest, and some special toys to help him develop his motor skills. He also got a package of new diapers from his practical grandparents.

Stan got fishing equipment, and a Harley-Davidson helmet. He also got Harley-Davidson socks, Harley-Davidson underwear, and a Harley-Davidson tie.

"You can ride my bike as long as you wear your helmet," Sara volunteered.

"How do you like the ashtray I made you in school?" Sean asked his father.

"I love it, son. But I don't smoke."

Shirley smiled. She'd been the recipient of numerous ashtrays, crafted by well-meaning children, over the years.

"Oh, yeah, you don't smoke," Sean said, as if the revelation just dawned on him. "But you can put it on your desk to hold all your papers."

"I can. It will go perfectly with the paperweight Samantha made me a few years ago."

"But mine is in the shape of a Harley, can't you tell?"

Stan held the black blob of pottery up. "It sure is. I'll keep it on my desk to remind me that the real thing is on its way—one of these days. Anyway, I'll be dressed for a long ride."

"We thought we had better start buying you the Harley-Davidson accessories now," Shirley said. "The call saying your Harley is in could come any time."

"I'm a patient boy," grinned Stan. "Don't worry about me. Besides, I see a lot of Harleys on the road lately. I think the supply and demand issue is dying out. If I walked into the shop now, I could probably buy a new one right off the floor."

"No kidding?"

"No kidding. My name came up a long time ago. I just told the salesman that I'd have to wait a little while longer, just until we win the lotto."

"I'm sorry, hon."

"Don't be. I've got everything right here that I need to make me the happiest man in the world."

Shirley opened her presents slowly. Somehow she felt she had already gotten more than she deserved. The lights on the house were still her favorite gift. But Stan and the kids did give her a journal and a day-planner.

"Now you can write down your innermost thoughts and feelings, and you won't have to take them out on us," Stan teased her.

"Just what I need," she said. "Thanks, everyone."

Stan made a roaring fire and burned up the mounds of wrapping paper that Sean had crushed with his prized monster truck.

Stan salvaged a white envelope. "I think this is yours," he said, extending it to Shirley. "It's got your name on it."

She immediately recognized the handwriting as her mother's.

The card simply read: "You should learn to listen to your mother. After all, I lived through the Cabbage Patch Doll craze with Sami, remember?"

Shirley remembered, all right. The mystery of the blue Monster Mountain Masher was solved.

Shirley went up to the solitude of her bedroom and dialed Lena's number. They had one of the best talks they had ever had. It was another present that couldn't be gift-wrapped.

After breakfast, Stan explained to the family that everyone was now going to help feed families that had no homes and no Christmas.

All of the children seemed to understand.

The shelter was not the one Shirley usually went to. This was the city's biggest facility. Today it was packed with families and individuals who had little reason to celebrate. Both Pat and Rita were already there and busy. They quickly put Shirley's family to work, serving food, cleaning up dishes, and making the people feel welcome.

Sara sang Christmas songs and the whole cafeteria joined in on "Jingle Bells." Shirley noticed that Sara seemed to have made friends with a little red-headed girl about her age.

Samantha, to her mother's surprise, seemed to fit in as easily as Rita. She didn't worry about how to serve people, she just served them. Shirley watched proudly as Samantha wiped tables, scraped plates, and talked to people. Everything she was always too sick to do at home.

Stan and Sean moved tables and chairs and helped with the heavier work.

Shirley carried Stephen in a backpack, which left her hands free to dish up turkey, potatoes, gravy, canned corn, and cranberry sauce.

There were a lot of volunteers there to help, but there were a lot more people who were on the receiving end, and Shirley couldn't help but wonder what would happen to them tomorrow, once Christmas was over.

When everyone had been fed and the area cleaned, no one in Shirley's family seemed eager to leave. Sara was playing with her new friend. Sean and a skinny boy about his age were having a blast with Sean's new Monster Mountain Masher. Sami was chatting with an entire family who had been left homeless after a flood. Stephen was sound asleep on Shirley's back.

For a while, Shirley lost track of Stan—until she heard a hearty, "Ho! Ho! Ho!"

He came out of the back room wearing a makeshift Santa suit, and began passing out the toys Rita had purchased at the mall. Every recipient appeared sincerely grateful, but none were as happy as Stan seemed.

On the way home Shirley felt her feelings roller-coaster between gratitude and guilt, but it was Stan who seemed the most affected by the experience.

"I imagine you're feeling a little overwhelmed," she said. "Like I did the first time Rita took me to the shelter."

"We have so much," he said slowly, steering their van around a corner. "Those people have so little. I used to think people were homeless because they were lazy, or did something stupid to bring on their own troubles. That's just not true. I met one man who was there because his wife had lost a long drawn-out battle with cancer. It wiped them out financially. After she died, he and his daughter ended up at the shelter."

Shirley wasn't sure what to say. "I believe every one of those people followed a path to that shelter, but none of them chose that path freely."

"I think you're right," Stan said. "And I think there is something more that we can do to help them."

He pulled the car over to the side of the road and stopped. Then Stan turned and looked at his family. "I remember a particular Christmas when I was a boy. My parents asked all of us to choose our favorite Christmas gift. We did. I picked a BB gun that I loved. My little brother picked a basketball signed by Dr. J.—Julius Erving.

"Then Daddy told us about a family on the other side of town with two boys, but no mother. Their father had just been laid off from the same company Daddy worked for. They had no money. No job. No Christmas."

"What happened to them?" asked Sara.

"Well, honey, my mother packed a few boxes with food. Dad stuffed some money in an envelope. My brother and I took that BB gun and basketball, and we gave that family a sort of

Christmas. I remember how hard it was, but mostly, I remember how that boy's face lit up like a Christmas bulb when I handed him that gun. It's always been tucked in the back of my mind, as one of my most priceless memories."

Shirley didn't mention it, but she had seen Stan empty his wallet at the shelter. She had seen Stan hand that homeless father all of the cash he was carrying. It had made Shirley proud, but being the cynic she was, Shirley had watched closely, making certain that Stan was giving his money away voluntarily, and not at knife-point.

"Why don't we go home and pick some presents and things we can give to those kids and families at the shelter?" Stan suggested. "I know it won't be much, but we could all stand to think a little more about giving, and not so much about getting."

Shirley waited for all of the children to volunteer their matching pajamas, but no one said anything.

Then Shirley turned to see Sara sniffling, her shoulders shaking.

"What's wrong, sweetie?"

"I left my new dolly at the shelter." Sara broke into full blown sobs.

"That's okay," Stan said gently. "We can get it when we go back there."

"No," said Sara. "I left it there on purpose. I gave it to my friend. She doesn't have a doll."

The reality of the moment dawned slowly, but profoundly.

Samantha was no longer wearing her new Christmas vest. She had left it at the shelter—had given it away to a girl she'd met there.

And Sean? Shirley looked to be sure, but he was not carrying his prized blue Monster Mountain Masher. His face was streaked with dried tears, but his smile taught them all, that it was truly more blessed to give than to receive.

That night when the family was all sleeping, Shirley sat in the rocking chair by a fireplace glowing with red embers. This was her favorite time. Her quiet time. *Her* time.

She held her journal in her lap and jotted down a few new year's resolutions. To always remember the lessons she'd learned this Christmas season, was at the top of her list.

The house was still strewn with wrapping paper and scattered Christmas presents. For some reason the mess didn't bother Shirley. She just sat there rocking. Thinking. Feeling

Quietly Shirley slipped from the chair and fell to her knees.

"Thank you," she prayed.

Shirley felt a warm, peaceful feeling envelope her, and for the first time all season, Shirley was filled with the *true* spirit of Christmas.

Don't miss these other *Shirley You Can Do It!* Books coming from Toni Sorenson Brown:

TURN THE PAGE FOR A SNEAK PREVIEW OF

Validate Me Quick;
I'm Double-Parked!

FOLLOWED BY AN EXCERPT FROM

In My Quest for Personal Growth,
The Rest of Me Grew, Too!

Validate Me Quick; I'm Double-Parked!

There had been no more 5:00 A.M. wake-up calls, but the metamorphosis of Shirley was definitely under way. While the outside remained the same, she could feel a transformation taking place within. Those deep rumblings of her spirit were frightening and at the same time, exhilarating. What would the "validated" Shirley be like, she wondered?

There were moments when she failed to suppress, but actually addressed, her hopes and fears with unharnessed imagination. That's when she saw herself happy, laughing carefree with her head back. That's when she saw herself thin. As long as she was shedding the shackles of unworthiness, she might as well shed some of the extra weight she carried underneath her clothes. She had seen overweight people on talk shows and they seemed happy with their big bodies and their broad lives. Still, whenever Shirley allowed her imagination to soar, the picture she painted of herself was always a little thinner than the one she saw when she looked in the mirror.

The "fantasy Shirley" was also surrounded by a happy family in a clean house.

Reality always reared its dubious head and brought Shirley right back to the sticky kitchen table that was capable of claiming your elbows if you set them down for too long. Somewhere between fantasy and reality, there had to be a world where Shirley could find validation.

If Stan and the kids suspected the change that was under way, they gave no indication. They seemed happy in their oblivion.

Cold cereal and white toast—actually, anything that could pop from the toaster—sufficed for breakfast. No one seemed to miss the "feathers" in the orange juice or the steaming cracked wheat cereal.

The minimum weekly exercise requirements Shirley had set for herself were sometimes met and sometimes let go.

She kept a little journal, but found that if she attempted to chart her progress on a daily basis, it was too disheartening. However, if she allowed herself some time and space, Shirley could see that she was headed in the right direction.

Maybe she just needed to stay pointed forward and keep moving. Perhaps this validation thing was as silly as it seemed at times.

Maybe this whole thing was not necessary, she about had herself convinced.

Then the doorbell rang.

"Mom! I was just thinking about you—sort of."

Lena half-hugged her daughter. "That's nice, I suppose." Then she quickly pushed past Shirley. Lena was wearing wearing a black skirt and a bright-yellow jacket. High heels. Shirley still had on her pajama bottoms, but at least they were mostly covered by one of Stan's old flannel shirts.

"I was in town for a doctor's appointment. I thought I'd stop by and see the children. Where are they?"

Lena looked around the kitchen and focused on the table. It was still covered with breakfast dishes, although it was practically lunch-time. Good thing Shirley had eaten the last blueberry Pop-Tart and had tossed the package into the garbage. Now the only evidence of Shirley's malnourished family was a spilled box of Cap'n Crunch.

Shirley tried to ignore the sneer that she was sure she saw register on Lena's face. Shirley almost always kept the house clean and orderly, but not on the days her mother popped in. Did the woman have spies?

"Mom, it's Wednesday. You know the kids are at school. Now, what did you say about a doctor's appointment? What's the matter? Are you sick?"

"Don't worry, dear," Shirley's mother answered, gingerly picking up a half-eaten Pop-Tart Shirley had missed. Lena dropped it onto a dirty plate and then stepped back, as if it were a grenade about to explode. "So where's little Sara?"

Shirley could not help it. She followed her mother's lead like a well-trained pet. She started cleaning the kitchen table, piling all of the partially eaten breakfast treats onto a plate and then into the garbage. She scooped the spilled Cap'n Crunch into a pile with Stan's shirtsleeve and then closed the box. She wanted to justify the mess by informing her mother that she had been upstairs working at the computer all morning. She wasn't lazy. She wasn't dirty. She wasn't worthless. Instead she looked at Lena. "Sara is at a neighbor's, playing. Tell me about your doctor's appointment."

"Do you have a dishcloth—a *clean* one?" Her mother avoided the question with a question.

Shirley felt the muscles in her neck tighten. This tug-of-war was an all too familiar game they played. Shirley always lost.

Not this time. She took a deep breath and tried to relax her tension. Then she handed her mother a fresh rag from the bottom drawer by the sink. "Have at it, Mom. Knock yourself out."

Fifteen minutes later, the kitchen was nearly clean, and Shirley and Lena had one more mother-daughter battle behind them.

"Why didn't you just tell me you were in town for your annual mammogram, Mom? Why did you have to worry me like that?"

"Worrying you is precisely what I was trying to avoid."

"Whatever."

"The first thing I told you was not to worry. Why are you on the defensive today, Shirley? You're not pregnant, are you?"

Shirley felt her neck muscles constrict again. "No. I'm not pregnant. Now, sit down."

"Excuse me?"

"Please, Mom. Have a seat. There is something I would like to talk to you about." Shirley decided there would never be a perfect time to get this validation thing under way, so she might as well take advantage of this time alone with her mother.

Lena rinsed the dishcloth and wiped the chair down while Shirley went to her bedroom. When she returned, she was carrying an envelope.

"What's this, a new diet?"

Shirley bit her lip until she could taste blood. "No, Mom. But it is going to help me get rid of some extra baggage." With that snappy comment Shirley suddenly realized she was on her own. Those $3.95 minutes had been a rip-off. No one had told Shirley *how* to seek validation.

"What is this—one of Sara's projects?"

"Nope. It's one of mine. It's my validation puzzle."

"Your what?" Lena sounded both confused and impatient. The way she always sounded when she wasn't so sure she had the upper hand.

"It's my attempt to feel validated by the people in my life who take me for granted. You know, I just want to feel acknowledged and appreciated."

"Don't we all?" Lena mumbled, but Shirley wasn't listening to anything except the pounding thunder of her own heart.

Shirley sat next to her mother at the now sparkling kitchen table and simply blurted out her deepest harbored feelings. She said something she had wanted to say to her mother ever since she was a child. "I hate buttermilk!"

Lena simply stared at her daughter for the longest minute of Shirley's life, then in that what's-wrong-with-you-now tone, she said, "Shirley, you're just having a very bad day."

The 1-900 number or not, she met her mother's gaze. "No, Mom. I'm actually having a pretty good day. Not an easy one, but a good one. There are just a few things I want you to know. Most of all, I love you. I really do. I know when Daddy walked out, you had to shoulder all of the responsibility of raising me. I don't pretend to know what that has been like for you, but I want you to know that I love you for it.

"I think we're a lot alike, Mom. But I am not you. I don't wash the dishes before I put them in the dishwasher. What's the point? I don't wear lipstick before noon. Okay, so there was that one time, but I'm not a high heels and ruby-red lips kind of woman. I buy my Thanksgiving rolls frozen in a plastic bag. I'm afraid of the sewing machine, Mom. Afraid of it, do you hear me?" Shirley had to pause to catch her breath.

Lena was no longer looking like a Supreme Court Justice, more like a distressed captive, eyeing the distance to the door. But Shirley was on a roll and couldn't allow herself to stop now.

"Mom, I'm very well aware of the fact that I'm overweight. You're not. I'm not a calorie counter like you. I think I'm more like one of those women who calories can count on. I'm fat and I know it, so there is no need for you to remind me every time we are together."

Another long and awkward pause seemed like it would never end. Then Shirley's mother asked quietly, "Is that it?"

"Did I mention that I detest buttermilk?"

"Yes, dear. You did."

"Okay, I guess that's it, then."

"My turn now?"

Shirley hesitated. "Fair's fair. Go for it, Mom."

"I love you, too. Really I do. More than you can know. Sometimes I say the wrong things. Sometimes I do things that hurt you. I'm truly sorry for those times. It's just that we are so different—"

"Exactly!" agreed Shirley. "We're alike, but different. Mom, you are a walking tradition. I'm a tradition breaker."

"That's one of the things I like about you," confessed Shirley's mother.

Just hearing her mother pinpoint something she "liked" about her made Shirley feel good.

The next silence that followed was the longest one. But no words were needed as mother and daughter embraced in the most spontaneous hug they had ever experienced.

Shirley was positive she had finally broken through. Her mother loved her and accepted her for what she was. This validation stuff really was a breeze.

Shirley's mother was the first to back away from the hug. "May I ask you something while we are being so open with each other?"

"Sure, Mom." Shirley had not felt this close to her mother since she was ten years old. "Ask me anything." But even as she invited the query, she also braced herself. Conditioned response or instinct. Either way, Shirley's defenses went up.

"What's with all the 'S' names in your family?" Lena asked.

Shirley stared at her mother. "What's that supposed to mean?" She could feel a week's growth of hair on her legs and under her arms, bristling.

"Nothing. Nothing at all." Her mother backed down. "I've just wondered about the novelty of it and I've never dared ask before."

"So are you saying you don't like our kids' names?"

"No, that's not what I'm saying at all. I have just wondered, if your name was Zenith and Stan's name was Zeus, would all your kids have 'Z' names?"

"Maybe. Would that affect how you felt about them?"

"Shirley, you're ruining our bonding moment. You're being silly now. I was just curious, that's all. I'm sorry I offended you. But have you ever stopped to think that your mother might need, might even deserve, validation, too? I like to be included. Consulted, even. It's no fun making a child your whole life only to have that child grow up and exclude you from her adulthood."

"I'm sorry, Mom. I never knew you felt excluded. I am sorry." Shirley's apology was sincere.

They spent the next thirty minutes learning things about each other that neither had suspected. Then Sara came home and Grandma went out to watch her Rollerblade. Shirley finished the document that was due the next day. Then she dumped a can of soup over some skinless chicken breasts and popped them in the Crock-Pot. She even changed into real clothes and did a once-over on her face.

"Do you want to stay and have supper with us?" Shirley invited her mother.

"No, I don't think so. For some reason, I feel like that wrung-out dishrag of yours. I think I'll go home, fix a salad, and then have a shower and go to bed."

"Sounds like a great idea," said Shirley. "Except for the salad part," she joked.

"A salad or two might be good for—" Lena could not help herself.

Shirley put her finger on her lips and shook her head. "Shhh . . . shhh. Don't spoil this bonding moment."

So, what exactly had happened?, Shirley wondered. Now what was she supposed to do with that first piece of the puzzle? Had her mother actually validated her? Lena had acknowledged the fact that Shirley's feelings were justified; they'd even discussed the value of their diversity. But still, Shirley was a little unsure. It seemed there should be more. There was more. Maybe there was always more.

Validation does work both ways, Shirley was thinking when the telephone rang.

"Shirley, it's me, your mother."

"Hi, Mom. I recognized your voice."

"That's a good sign, I suppose. Anyway, listen to this. Yesterday when I got home I watched an *Oprah* episode, and guess what it was about?"

"Men who love women who are really men?"

"No, no. You've got Jenny Jones mixed up with Oprah. Oprah has gone higher class now that she's got the power. Of course her ratings have dropped, but she doesn't do trash TV anymore."

"So what was the program about?"

"Validation! Can you believe it—validation!"

"No kidding?"

"I tried to tape it for you, but you know I still don't know how to push those two buttons on the VCR at once. I don't understand why you can't just push Record. It makes no sense, does it?"

"Life's complicated, Mom, but you're wandering. Tell me what Oprah had to say about validation."

"You'll have to watch the rerun, Shirley. I only caught part of it, but she said the same thing you said. We all need to be recognized for what we contribute. We need to feel appreciated. We need to feel like we matter."

"Amen."

"I've been thinking about something you said, Shirley. You and I are really not all that different."

Shirley smiled as she nestled the telephone receiver between her chin and shoulder so her hands were free to wipe the kitchen counters. The kitchen table was already clean. "I thought we established that yesterday, Mom. We have a lot of similarities, but also a lot of differences."

"Exactly." Lena sounded pleased. "We agree on more than you realize. I have a confession."

Shirley tossed the dishcloth into the sink and held the receiver so she could hear clearly. "What kind of a confession, Mother?"

Lena laughed. "Nothing major. It's just that I hate buttermilk, too."

Shirley was shocked. "Then why on earth do you guzzle it by the quart? And why did you make me?"

"Because when I was a girl, my mother drank it and she made me. You don't know what gross is until you drink warm buttermilk. I guess you do what you get used to. But listen to this—I called my mother this morning and asked her, 'Why all the buttermilk?' You'll never guess what she said."

"So tell me."

"In her day and age, they didn't have electric refrigerators. They had iceboxes. I remember those iceboxes. Shirley, your generation is spoiled. You take it for granted that when you flip a switch a light will come on. When you want a cold drink, you open the fridge. It hasn't been that long ago that—"

"Mom, you're rambling."

"I'm sorry, dear. Where was I?"

"Buttermilk."

"Right." Lena paused long enough to gather her thoughts. "This open communication thing between us is so new, Shirley. You're just going to have to be patient with me if I get ahead of myself."

"No problem, Mom."

"Okay. Well, you know your grandmother, my mother, was raised on a farm. They milked their own cows morning and night. Nothing was wasted back then. The Great Depression, you know. So they had to hurry and drink the buttermilk they made before it spoiled. Turns out Mother hates the nasty stuff, too. It's just that her mother made her drink it and so she made me and I made you and don't you dare make Samantha or Sara."

"I couldn't even if I tried." Shirley laughed, feeling that the first piece of her puzzle now fit perfectly.

In My Quest for Personal Growth, The Rest of Me Grew, Too!

Shirley was ten minutes late picking Sara up from preschool.

"Did you forget about me, Mommy?"

"Of course not, sweetie. I just got *stuck* at the mall." The thought made Shirley smile.

"I made a surprise for you for Mother's Day," Sara announced proudly.

Shirley grinned. "Really? What is it?"

"I can't tell. It's a surprise."

"Those are my favorite Mother's Day presents," Shirley lied, like any good mother would.

Later that night, after macaroni-and-cheese casserole *again*, and after the kids received their gifts from her impromptu guilt-driven shopping spree, Shirley lay on top of her bed, too tired to get off, pull down the covers and crawl in properly. Every inch of her body ached. Screamed for relief. She reached for the box of turtles she had given Stan.

"How did your doctor's appointment go?" Stan asked, flopping down on the bed just hard enough to jolt every one of Shirley's just-beginning-to-relax muscles.

"Everything's right on target."

"No problems?"

His tone alarmed Shirley. "What do you mean?"

"I mean the water retention. Isn't that a concern?"

"I didn't know you were so aware of my water level." Her feeling of alarm quickly turned to annoyance. "I'm fine. Just pregnant."

"What about the irritability?"

"*What* irritability?" she snapped.

Stan reached for a chocolate, but Shirley snapped the lid closed.

After surviving three pregnancies, the man hadn't learned

a thing. "And what did the doctor say about your weight gain? Aren't they worried about high blood pressure?"

Shirley took a deep breath, or at least she tried to. Then her bare feet landed in the square of Stan's back. He was on the floor before he knew it.

"What was *that* all about?" He seemed genuinely bewildered as he staggered to his feet.

"Just chalk it up to my water retention, irritability, and weight gain!" she said, popping a whole turtle into her mouth.

Sometime after she fell asleep, the phone rang. And rang. And rang.

Finally someone picked it up, and somewhere in the depths of slumber, Shirley heard Stan bellow from downstairs, "Shirley, it's for you."

"Hello," Shirley muttered as she fumbled with the receiver.

"Hi, Shirley. It's Rita. I hope I didn't wake you."

It took at least ten seconds for Shirley to remember who Rita was. Then she looked at her clock on the nightstand. It was only 9:00 P.M. But it felt like it was 3:00 A.M. "Oh, no. I wasn't sleeping," Shirley lied.

"I just called to see if tomorrow would be a good day to take you up on your offer for lunch. My office is being painted and I'm all unpacked, so I thought . . ."

"Sure. Tomorrow sounds great." The idea of a lunch she didn't spread on a piece of bread brought Shirley to full-alert status. Besides, Rita was intriguing and Shirley was up for a little intrigue. "What if we meet at The Garden? It's a soup and salad place on Main Street."

"The Garden is fine, but why don't you let me come and pick you up? That way you won't have to worry about driving in your condition." Rita laughed, a little hesitantly. "I hope I didn't offend you."

"You didn't," Shirley assured her. "I don't take offense. I give it. Just ask my husband, Stan, who blames my snarly moods on my 'condition,' even when I'm not pregnant." She laughed at her own joke.

The next morning, Shirley got up early to clean the house. She swept the kitchen and bathroom floors and ran a wet mop over them. She washed dishes and put a fresh cloth on the kitchen table. She sprayed some floral potpourri and lit a cinnamon candle. She thought about vacuuming, but decided against it. No use going into labor before lunch.

Stan kissed her carefully on the cheek. "Good morning. It looks like you're getting serious about having this baby. You're nesting."

"I'm not nesting. I'm just cleaning. I want the house to look nice when my new friend gets here."

"You mean the woman who called you last night? Isn't she the one who pried you out of the revolving door?"

Why did Shirley have to tell him everything? It always came back to haunt her. "That's the one. We're going to lunch. So if you'll take Sara to preschool, I'll pick her up."

"Sure," said Stan. "No problem. I can even pick her up if you would like more time to spend with . . . what did you say your friend's name was?"

"Rita. And why are you being so nice?" she asked suspiciously, knowing that after her behavior last night, Stan did not need to be nice to her. She had apologized for kicking him in the back, but he had just laughed and blamed it on her "condition."

Now Stan picked up a wet dishcloth and ran it over the top of the fridge. "I'm not being nice. I'm just nesting. *We're* about to have a baby."

"Sometimes I love you," she said, backing into his chest because she couldn't manage a tight enough hug facing him.

He wrapped his arms nearly all the way around her and patted her stomach.

"I love you more today than I did yesterday," she said.

Stan kissed her neck. "Yeah, but yesterday you hated my guts!"

Lunch consisted of Jamaican black bean soup and all the iceberg lettuce you could eat.

"This is a quaint little cafe," said Rita, buttering a soda cracker with the real artery-clogging stuff.

"Charming, isn't it? You know, I didn't think you and I could ever be friends," Shirley confessed.

"Why?"

"Because you're too skinny. That's the first thing I noticed about you."

Rita laughed. "I presume you took note of my weight after you were freed from the revolving door. But actually, I'm not slender enough to be noticeable."

"No, I mean it. Call me prejudiced, but lately skinny people really *bug* me. Rickets isn't a contagious disease, is it?" Shirley teased.

Rita continued laughing. "Shirley, I might not be the best thing for you, but you certainly are a blessing to me."

Shirley had a million questions she wanted to ask Rita. Her natural curiosity demanded to know all the juicy details of Rita's life, including her briefly mentioned recent divorce. However, Rita was driving and Shirley wanted to make sure she still had a ride home. So she kept the queries simple.

"Why did you decide to settle here in our illustrious little city?"

"I do a lot of social work. Right now, I've decided to open a public relations firm for nonprofit organizations. The demographics here are favorable."

Shirley stuck a big spoonful of soup into her mouth, but her eyes still questioned, "Huh?" She suddenly felt very uneducated and small-town, so she followed the soup with a big bite of lettuce, thinking that if she kept eating, she would not say anything stupid in front of this woman who obviously was the epitome of sophistication. Shirley couldn't help feeling not only inferior, but somewhat envious.

"I guess what really drew me here," Rita's lip began to quiver as the model of sophistication fought to maintain her composure, "is the fact that I have absolutely no ties here. No ex-husbands and none of their mistresses. No coworkers who saw me fall apart. No family and no friends to keep reminding me that I have failed miserably at the most important ventures of my life."

Shirley wasn't sure whether or not a response was required. Did Rita say *husbands*? Shirley was dying to ask how many and all about those dissolved marriages, but suspected that what Rita really needed was not a barrage of questions, but simply a sounding board. So Shirley did what any true friend does—she listened.

It wasn't easy for Shirley, but she kept alternating bites of soup and chunks of lettuce, just to ensure her own silence, as Rita poured out her soul. She talked of a life of affluence and apocalypse. Deceit and disappointment. A princess broken. She spoke in general terms while Shirley craved details, but refrained from querying.

It was a life so foreign to Shirley that it might as well have been a work of fiction. A soap opera. But it wasn't. It was real. Rita was born into a family of old money and power. She was educated, traveled, and regal. But right now, she was on the brink of breaking down in front of a near-stranger.

Rita sniffled and wiped her eyes with the corner of her napkin. "I guess I'm evidence that money does not buy happiness."

Shirley had heard that line too many times. "From one who has six dollars and nine cents in her checking account, I'd say you just didn't know where to shop!"

"How was your lunch?" Stan asked early that evening while husband and wife were out on their weekly "get away from the kids" date. They were doing some joint grocery shopping.

"I can still taste it." Shirley burped. "Excuse me."

"Tell me about your friend Rita. She comes from money, huh?"

Shirley instantly felt defensive. "Yeah, but so what? There is a lot more to her than her bank account."

"Sorry. I didn't mean to imply anything derogatory."

"*I'm* sorry, hon. It's just that I feel Rita and I have been friends forever. It's one of those rare, rare connections. Kinda like you and me—the connection defies logic."

Stan helped Shirley lift a box of laundry detergent into their cart. "Should I be jealous?"

Shirley chuckled. "Hardly."

"So tell me about Rita," said Stan, trying to sneak a box of Twinkies into the cart without Shirley detecting them.

Shirley tossed a second box of Twinkies into the cart. "She is one of the warmest and funniest people I've ever met. After she stopped crying, we laughed until I almost peed my pants."

Stan muttered, "That wouldn't take much these days."

"What did you say?"

"I said I need something for lunch Tuesday."

Shirley gave him that sideways "Yeah, right" look, but continued her Rita story. "Her family is from the Northwest. They are spread between Seattle and Portland. She's been educated in the best schools in the U.S. and Europe. She's traveled the world. I think she married young. Her father really liked her first husband. I think it was one of those archaic forced unions."

"Her *first* husband?" Stan questioned, tossing a package of toilet paper at Shirley.

She caught it and threw it into the cart. "Yeah. I know she's been married at least twice."

"At *least*?"

"I know her last husband was a doctor who became more interested in the anatomy of student nurses than in anatomy in general. Can you believe men, it doesn't matter whether they are doctors or ditch-diggers, they're all the same."

Stan stood in front of a rack of two hundred loaves of bread, pretending to be perplexed by the variety. When Shirley finally stopped talking, he reached for a loaf of sourdough.

"So why *is* she here?" he asked.

Shirley lifted her shoulders. "I'm not sure. I suspect it's because this is an easy place in which to lose yourself."

Stan double-checked the shopping list. "How come you didn't write down any of the good stuff, like chips and dip or frozen pizzas?"

"Because I'm trying to diet."

"Which one is it this week, all grapefruit, whole grain, all protein, no sugar, no carbs, no taste?"

Shirley shook her head and returned the loaf of sourdough to the bread shelf. "No white bread."

Stan put it back in the cart. "Just because you're dieting, doesn't mean the rest of us are. I'm not sure it's a good idea for you to diet while you're pregnant anyway."

"It's nothing radical. Just a few smart choices to help me keep my weight under control."

Stan coughed. Or was it a snort?

"Are you laughing at me?"

He looked like a five-year-old caught with his hand in his mother's purse. "Why would I laugh at you?"

"Because maybe, just maybe, you think my pregnancy weight is *already* out of control." There were a few issues in Shirley's life that she was hypersensitive about—her weight covered the first five of the top-ten list.

"Shirl, don't worry at this point—just go ahead for the next few weeks and splurge. After the baby comes, we'll diet and exercise together."

After the baby comes . . .